PODS FOR PIGS

GORDON IAN MACLEOD

Front cover illustrated by Elaine Wood

Other Novels by Gordon MacLeod

Silicon Glen

76

Just a Little Drop More

Beyond the Tree at Mamre

Carrot Toppers

Short Stories

You Just Can't Cross a Rainbow (unpublished)

Plays

Absent Friends

44(1) (b)

Where Did All the Flowers Come From?

The Gatekeeper (unpublished)

A Haggis Sausage Roll (unpublished)

Radio Drama

On the Breadline

Screenplay/Film Script

Molios

© Copyright 2020 by Gordon MacLeod, all rights reserved.

No part of this publication may be reproduced, stored in a retrieval system, or transmitted, in any form or by any means, electronic, mechanical, photocopying, recording, or otherwise, without the written permission of the author.

http://gordonmacleod.weebly.com

Author's Note to the Reader

The events and characters in this novel are works of fiction and in no way represent real events.

Some place names may be real, however that is where all similarity ends.

PROLOGUE: THE CALL
CHAPTER 1: PIG PODS
CHAPTER 2: LIKE FATHER LIKE SON
CHAPTER 3: FRIENDS REUNITED
CHAPTER 4: ASSIGNATION
CHAPTER 5: THE LAST SUPPER
CHAPTER 6: THE MAN WITH NO NAME
CHAPTER 7: REIMAGINING THE FUTURE
CHAPTER 8: CRISIS MANAGEMENT
CHAPTER 9: HOMECOMING
CHAPTER 10: KNOCKDOWN
CHAPTER 11: LAMENTATIONS
CHAPTER 12: POTATO HEAD
CHAPTER 13: FEELINGS OF LOSS
CHAPTER 14: THE BIRDS
CHAPTER 15: WHEN THE BOAT COMES IN
CHAPTER 16: A PAIN IN THE BUTT
CHAPTER 17: THE UNOFFICIAL WAKE
CHAPTER 18: SUSPICIONS
CHAPTER 19: MORE SUSPICIONS
CHAPTER 20: GUILTY UNTIL PROVEN INNOCENT
CHAPTER 21: REVELATION
CHAPTER 22: ON-CALL
CHAPTER 23: THE BRIEF VISITATION
CHAPTER 24: THE RETURN LEG
CHAPTER 25: NIGHT OF THE VERY LONG FACES
CHAPTER 26: A DEAD WEIGHT
CHAPTER 27: THE RETURN OF THE KING
CHAPTER 28: MEAL TIME INTERRUPTIONS

CHAPTER 29: CEILIDH

THE CALL

It was mid-morning when both the Portree Lifeboat on the Isle of Skye, and the Scottish Ambulance service, were alerted to a medical emergency on the neighbouring island of Raasay.

James MacLeod, the Lifeboat Coxswain, was undaunted when he got the shout via a R.C.A.M.S. alert on his mobile phone.
He responded by pressing the tab marked yes on the screen, knowing that his fellow crew members would also be responding in a similar fashion, subject to their availability, using the new alert system which they had initially wrestled with following its introduction.

When he got to the pier, he observed two paramedics waiting at the lifeboat station.
They were holding an oxygen bottle with a face mask.
It must be a medical emergency, he thought.

He learned from them that they had been called to Inverarish, to pick up a female casualty in her 20's by the name of Nicolson.
She had been experiencing difficulty breathing.
Whether or not this was related to coronavirus, or something else, they were unsure of at this stage, but they advised James that they would undertake all the manual handling and care of the patient, to ensure any risk to the crew was minimized and two metres distance enforced.

This is the way how casualties are transported to the hospital quickly from Raasay, which had no hospital of its own, when the ferry was either unavailable, or deemed to be too slow.

It was not long before the crew had changed into their gear and their D class craft was being lowered by crane into the water. As they skimmed across the surface of a cold and dark blue choppy sea, they soon reached and boarded the rescue vessel, a Trent Class All- Weather lifeboat.

On arrival at Inverarish on the smaller island, they were met by the local fire crew.
Two of the local nurses were also in attendance.

James observed from the boat that the female casualty was walking, which he felt was a good sign.
The two paramedics carefully took the young woman onto the boat, with the crew keeping their distance on this occasion.
In little under a couple of minutes, they were making the return journey, skimming the white horses enroute to Portree.

On arrival, the paramedics walked slowly with her from the pierhead and into the ambulance, for transfer to A&E at Portree Hospital.
The Lifeboat crew hosed down the craft, and following the new infection control procedures, wiped down the surfaces with disinfectant wipes around where the casualty had been, in the event she had been carrying COVID.

PIG PODS

'I really don't know why you bother going, Sunday after Sunday', said Alex disparagingly. 'Soon no-one will even bother'.

John straightened himself from the waist up, looking into the mirror that hung above the mantlepiece and straightened his tie. He refused to rise to his elder son's challenge, for he had heard it said many a time before. Although there was some truth in what he was saying, he didn't concede the point.

'As you know, it's only once a *fortnight* Alex', he replied pointedly.

'Why you choose to go to an *English* Church, makes no sense to me,' Alex protested.

His father couldn't let that one go.

'You've no idea what you are talking about laddie', he retorted.

'Come on you two', interrupted his wife, in some forlorn attempt to maintain harmony within her household. But it was too late.

'Well explain it to me then, oh fountain of all knowledge', Alex interrupted sardonically.

'Again?' said his father disbelievingly. 'I really don't have time for this just now'.

'That's convenient', insisted Alex. There was a short pause.

'The Episcopal Church', John started sharply, but stopped. 'The *Scottish* Episcopal Church', he emphasized, 'is the original church in Scotland'.

'How do you work that one out then?' came his son's sarcastic reply.

'If you read your history books', his father suggested, 'you'd maybe know why'.

'They didn't teach us Scottish history at school Dad'.

'Well for a future schoolteacher, it'd be useful if you'd familiarize yourself with some', retorted John, just as sarcastically as his eldest son had mustered.

'Well go on then,' he invited.

'The Scottish Episcopal Church…'

'We got that one already', insisted Alex. His father glared at him for the unnecessary intrusion, and raised his voice.

'…is the guardian of the true faith in Scotland. The Scottish Bishops pledged their allegiance to King James, and refused to transfer their loyalty to William of Orange'.

'So how does that make them the original church in Scotland then?' Alex queried, beginning to show more interest in genuine debate.

'Well, because they refused to transfer their loyalties, the Crown, not surprisingly, decided that they'd no longer be recognised as the true Church in Scotland'.

'That's just what I was saying', sneered Alex.

'No, it's not', insisted his father, 'you will find that many Scottish Episcopalians joined the Jacobite uprising. In fact, if you go to Ballachulish, they say you can still see the Appin chalice, which the Jacobite Stewarts used for communion, the night before the battle of Culloden'.

'So how does your church even still exist then?' came the impertinent response.

'Well after the battle, true enough, the Episcopal Church was suppressed. But some Episcopalian chapels remained, and in the 19th Century, once the rules were relaxed, the chapels accepted oversight of the Scottish Episcopalian Bishops'.
Before he was greeted with another disbelieving reply, John headed for the door.
'Right, your mother and I will be back after mid-day'.

'Maybe you'd fire up the Aga for me at half eleven Alex?' his mother called, looking back towards her eldest son as she exited the small croft house door.

'But I'm going to see Fi…', but his protest was shut down as the door slammed, prematurely cutting off his voice.

Alex slumped back on to the sofa which barely fitted in the small lounge, and which doubled as a kitchen. He wondered how he and his younger brother had survived his childhood in such cramped conditions. The flat he shared with his mates in Edinburgh was far more spacious than this 'agrarian dump', as he often referred to it, when in their company.

He had only lain back down for several minutes, when the croft house door opened.
His younger brother, Malcolm, appeared in the doorway and went over to the Aga to warm himself.

'It's not very warm', he grumbled reversing his body up towards it.

'That's a point', gasped his elder brother Alex. 'Are you here for the next hour?'

'Sure, why?' asked Malcolm.

'Because the Oldies want us to fire it up for them about half eleven, but I need to go out in ten minutes', his elder brother informed.

'Sure…where you off to?' enquired Malcolm.

'To Fiona's. I said I'd go and see her this morning. She goes back to Uni tomorrow morning', he informed.

'Well, there's not much of the morning left', laughed Malcolm.

'Shut it!' said his brother laughing, producing the cushion from behind his back and launching it at his younger sibling.

Malcolm caught it, but before he could throw it back, Alex had sprung to his feet and had left the room. He had gone through to the bedroom which they still shared, when he was home from University. Malcolm started to rake out the ash from the peat fire, while trying to retain what embers were left for lighting the new peats that lay in the basket beside the big iron stove.

He laughed when he put the new peat on the embers and opened out the fire, as he got a whiff of the peat up his nostrils. It made him think on how people would now pay for that privilege. It was only a few months until the new distillery would be producing its first single malt whisky, or as many on the island were quick to say under their breath, the first *'legal'* whisky. They were all keenly waiting in anticipation, the tasting of that first peaty dram from their island home.

His thoughts were interrupted as Alex reappeared having thrown on a jumper and a pair of jeans.

'I don't know why they don't move with the times and get an electric cooker. It's such a bloody mess all that', said the elder lifting his nose in the air as he adjusted the collar, and as he watched Malcolm balance a tray of ashes on the end of the riddling tool.

'I think Mum likes it for cooking, and it provides the central heating', Malcolm suggested. But his brother's lukewarm response symbolized what he thought of its heat generating abilities, as he headed towards the croft house door.

'Right, I'm off to see Fiona. I'll be back by two'.

'Okay, catch you later. Say hi to Fiona for me', the younger shouted as Alex exited the small white croft house and shut its door firmly behind him.

It took him no more than twenty minutes to reach Fiona's house at Inverarish Terrace. Although the houses were small, at least they were built in the 20th century, he thought. He walked up past the community run shop and post office, and went around the corner.
Knocking on the door of the little terraced house, he surveyed the surroundings as he waited for the door to open. Across the road lay the row of small gardens and outbuildings which were situated opposite each property. The door opened.

Without a word, an older woman took one look at him, turned and shouted up the stairs,

'Fiona, that's Alex for you'.

And although the whole village would have probably heard that, he found it amusing how probably ten years ago, when they all would play together and come to each other's door, the greeting would have been exactly the same then, just as it was now.
Nothing changes, he thought to himself, and that, he concluded, is just what the problem is.

Once her mother turned around and had gone back inside to attend to whatever it was she had been doing beforehand, Fiona appeared in the doorway.

'Hi', she said.

'Hi', he replied. 'Do you want to go a walk?' he invited.

'Maybe later', she said quietly, 'it's Sunday. Why don't you come in. We can go upstairs?'

'Och you're as bad as that lot at my house', he snorted.

'Oh', she replied a little taken aback, but sensed his agitation. 'Okay, we'll go a short one'.

Fiona was a year younger than him. She too was at studying in Glasgow to go into Primary School teaching. She was smaller than him, but was very attractive facially. Maybe a bit 'frumpy', as he had described her to his flat mates, before they met her for the first time. He had said she was a bit like 'the girl next door'. In fact, he was beginning to doubt whether or not there was much value in the relationship. She seemed content with island life, and aspired to come back as the teacher to the local Primary school on Raasay.

'Oh, that would all just work out perfectly Alex', she had said in a dreamy kind of way, when they had both gone to the mainland to study for their respective careers.
'You could be a teacher at the High School in Portree', she had decided, 'and we can stay here at home on the island'.

She collected her jacket from the row of pegs that ran along the wall beside the front door. They walked past the row of houses with their little gardens across the road, and turned down towards the old Mill.

'Let's go into the Park', he suggested nodding with his head towards the gated entrance.

'We can't', she protested.

'Why not?' he laughed mockingly.

'Because it's Sunday Alex', she informed.

'For God's sake Fiona, grow up!' he exclaimed.

'It's not me that needs to grow up. Look it's right there in front of you', she said pointing to the sign.

'That's for the old folk Fiona. *Don't use this playing field on Sundays.* What do you think is going to happen to us? The ground is going to open up and swallow us? We'll be struck down by some plague, eh?' he jeered mockingly.

'Don't make fun of me Alex', she gasped, rummaging around in her pocket frantically for something.

'Well, it really is so stupid. It's the 21st century for God's sake'.

She put an inhaler into her mouth and took a deep inward breath before spluttering out her disapproval.

'It's about…', she coughed. 'It's about being respectful', she insisted, trying again to complete her sentence.

'Respectful to who Fiona? Respectful to who exactly?'

'Respectful to God, respectful to the people here Alex. Respectful to a way of life', she retorted angrily.

'The way of life', he mocked. 'What life?' he asked pointedly.

'The life you and I grew up in and will hopefully return to once Uni is over Alex'.

'I'm beginning to wonder if that's not some kind of hell on earth', he said despondently.

'What? Do you mean with me Alex?' she asked accusingly.

'No that's not what...', he tried to explain, but the damage was done.

'Well, I can't say I haven't seen it coming Alex MacLean. You're no better than a pig', she cried.

He laughed which only served to make her even more angry.

'A pig that takes advantage of people!' she hollered, turning on her heels and storming off.

He thought about going after her. He hadn't meant to laugh. He had just been unsure what to say, as he was not used to being challenged by her.

He walked back along the road, but did not follow her up Inverarish Terrace, but instead carried on walking down the road towards the old pier at Suisnish.

Passing the war monument, a memorial to those from the island who had been lost in the two world wars, he continued on until he rounded a slight bend on the road. This then opened up a magnificent vista across the Sound of Raasay, with the Cuillins, a mountain range on the neighbouring island of Skye, casting their reflection on the water.

Meandering his way along the Shore Road, he noticed how the cliff face was crumbling, with more small landslips than he had ever seen before. He hadn't walked down the road for several months now, the last occasion being before he left the island for the start of the new academic year in September. He was sure there was more erosion now than there had been then. The island was crumbling before his very eyes. That's appropriate, he thought. He observed how the sea level was also beginning to erode a little of the road, and wondered how long it would be before that part fell away into the sea.

He laughed aloud like a mad man. The irony, he thought to himself. An island famous for road building, and the road is falling apart. He smiled at the thought. And although it was only a little erosion, he turned around before he got to the old Pier, and started to walk back towards the little croft house which he found increasingly claustrophobic. Perhaps it was time for a change. He felt his surroundings were squeezing the life out of him. I'm dying here, he concluded and resolved to do something about it.

Arriving home, having stopped off for some reason to look at the Fountain Pond which lay in the grounds of Raasay House, home of the former Clan Chief, and which now was a hotel and outdoor centre, he found the garden around the pond was badly overgrown. He noted that his parents' car was in the driveway. He opened the front door remembering to duck as he entered, having outgrown the height of the entrance many years ago, when he had reached his teenage years.

'Hello Alex', his mother greeted him, as she stood over the large cast iron stove, stirring the large pot of soup which she had made earlier.

He was still feeling irritated, not so much about his disagreement with Fiona, but more so that the Fountain Pond Garden had been left to overgrow, so much so that it was barely recognisable anymore and much less easy to find.

'You know the pond with the fountain at the Big House?' he remarked.

'No, I'm not so sure I do', said his mother slowly, while thinking hard about his question and the contents of the soup simultaneously.

'Yes, you do', he said in an irate manner.

'Well, if I do dear, I don't remember it', she said calmly in response.

'Yes, you do', Alex insisted.

'Well, if you insist dear, but I just don't recollect it.

'Yes, you do. Remember the one all the school children and the Friends Group worked on, which you told us about when we were younger? You were one of them'. He shook his head in despair.

'Oh, *that* garden', she concluded. 'What about it?'

'Oh, never mind'.

Alex went through to the small bedroom that still had the bunk beds he and his brother Malcolm had slept in from when they were younger, or much to his disgust, still slept in when he was home from University. The house lacked privacy, it was too small, and you could still see where the drain had run from inside the house to the outside, from a time when crofters took their cattle in for shelter. Thank God it still wasn't that primitive, he consoled himself, though it was primitive enough as far as he was concerned.

Malcolm came in and interrupted his thoughts.

'Mum says dinner is ready', he informed.

'Just coming', advised Alex, but also enquiring from his younger brother, 'what have you been up to?'

'Och I was just uncovering the Arran Pilots from their trays, as the potatoes will be ready for chitting soon'.

'Oh', said Alex in disgust, having just had his idea of a primitive agrarian lifestyle confirmed to him again.

Alex followed his younger brother, whom he felt sorry for, into the living room cum kitchen.

'No-one can beat your soup', his father was busy telling his mother, who had just placed a large plate of it in front of her husband.

Both boys took a seat and were served in similar fashion, before his mother joined them at the table.

'Let us pray', said his father.

They all duly bowed their heads, except for Alex, who sat impatiently rolling his eyes, while his Dad gave a rendition of the Selkirk Grace.

'Some hae meat and canna eat
And some would eat that want it;
But we hae meat and we can eat
And sae the Lord be thankit'.

'Burns', mused Alex.

'Burns indeed', said his father. 'There is no finer', he added.

'I'm surprised you'd use the words of a lowlander, and a poem that comes from the Borders', Alex remarked.

'I'll use the words of anyone who speaks sense', his father affirmed.

'Come on you two', interrupted his mother, 'let's just try and eat peacefully'. And with that she changed the conversation.

'So how was Fiona?' she asked. 'She's such a fine lass', she added approvingly.

'Well, she wasn't feeling that fine when I saw her', Alex informed.

'Oh, and why was that then?' his mother enquired.

'I don't think we quite see eye to eye mother'.

'Eye to eye, on what exactly?' she asked pursuing the matter further.

'I think she lacks ambition', he stated emphatically.

'Ambition?' his mother queried, her voice rising as she did so.

'Yes, ambition, drive – drive to better yourself', suggested Alex.

'Nonsense dear!' his mother exclaimed. 'Why she's looking at taking Mrs. MacLeod's job next year when she retires'.

'*If* she gets it', Alex insisted quickly, 'and even if she does, that's all she wants out of life'.

'Well, I think that is a lot', his father interjected. 'There are many people nowadays, trapped in zero hours contracts and casual labour. What do they call it?'

'The gig economy Dad', clarified Alex.

'Yes, the gig economy. Things are going backwards to an age that should be past, rather than forwards', he suggested. 'Getting a professional occupation and holding onto it is a major achievement these days son'.

'Maybe so', said Alex, 'but living here on the island. There's little future'.

'I'm not so sure son', his father said, rebutting his son's negativity. 'There's the distillery that is providing employment for local people. In fact, we even grew some of the barley for it ourselves last year'.

'Exactly, that's my point Dad. What future is there for younger people in that?' proposed Alex.

'Well, your brother manages fine on the croft. Don't you Malcolm?' his father asked rhetorically.
'It's all about thinking creatively', he continued.

'Creatively?' said Alex, the contempt dripping from his tongue.

'Yes, it's all about diversification', his father stated.

'So, asides from growing barley for the Distillery, what *diversity* is there in a crofting way of life Dad?'

'Well, only last week I decided that we will site a few pods on our land and take in campers over the holiday seasons of the year'.

'What do you mean, glamping?' his eldest son asked.

'Yes similar, look I'll show you. I got the idea from a newspaper which I kept'.

His father rose from the table and rummaging in a magazine rack, returned with a newspaper. His put it down on the table in front of his elder son. Alex looked at him alarmed.

'See, there you are', said his father.

'But Dad, these are pig pods', said Alex in disgust.

'Yes, I know that's what they are called, but they are for campers'.
'But *pods are for pigs* Dad!' his son shouted in derision.

'Yes, but they do well down south, and you can fit a double bed in them, and even turn them into an office if you were so minded', his father said, concluding his case.

'Pods… for pigs! Jesus Christ Dad', cursed his son.

'Now enough of that', his mother interrupted, and the rest of the soup dish was taken in silence.

As Alex lay there that night on the top bunk, he debated with himself whether or not he should go down and see Fiona off on the ferry in the morning. She'd need to get the early twenty past eight ferry to get to Glasgow at a decent hour, around four o'clock that afternoon. He was still caught up in disbelief that his parents and brother were going to have glamping on the croft land. As he lay there thinking about it and counting pigs in his mind, he drifted off into a deep sleep.

He lapsed in and out of sleep during the night, as the tiles on the roof were lifting in the strong south westerly gale which engulfed the small croft house. It was not unusual to have storms, particularly at this time of year.

LIKE FATHER LIKE SON

When Alex awoke later in the morning, he realized it was too late. Fiona would already have left on the early ferry. He really didn't care. He strained his neck to look down into the bunk below, but his brother had already left the house.

The bath was lukewarm and Alex returned to the bedroom feeling much colder than when he had left it. After drying himself, he got dressed and started packing his clothes into his holdall. He would be tracing the same path the next day, that Fiona had trod earlier that morning. His classes restarted the following day, and he had to return the day before to ensure he was available for them. Always having to leave early to catch the ferry was yet another disadvantage of island life, he reasoned to himself, feeling a moment of gladness at the thought of getting off his island prison.

As he walked into the main village headlong into the wind, he hoped to pick up a 'Herald' newspaper. At least it was his last day, and he'd feel a bit more re-orientated to city culture reading through the newspaper. Returning to Oscaig, he stuck to the road that ran behind Raasay House, and he stopped for a moment at the bottom of the hillock upon which sat St. Moluag's Chapel. Whether or not there was any truth in it or not he did not know, but he had heard it said when he was younger, that in some of the islands his name was invoked as a cure for madness. Alex felt he would need one if he had to stay on the island one moment longer than was necessary.

It was a cold morning due to the south westerly gale that was blowing. He thought that Fiona must have had a pretty bumpy ride across on the ferry that morning. 'Hallaig' as it was called, was the diesel electric hybrid passenger ferry that ran between the island and Sconser on Skye. He wasn't too concerned that the strong breeze would delay him tomorrow, as usually there was a period of calm following on from a gale.

Lost in his thoughts, he approached the croft house and almost literally bumped into his brother.

'Is that you back from seeing Fiona off?' he asked.

'No, I missed her', said Alex, not too concerned.

'That's a shame', said Malcolm. 'You should have asked me to wake you when I got up'.

'I'm not that bothered', insisted Alex as he shrugged his shoulders. 'What were you doing up so early this morning anyway?'

'I was up moving the hen house', Malcolm informed.

'Why did you move the hen house?' asked Alex feigning interest.

'The storm', informed Malcolm. 'It's only going to get a lot worse. You better keep a watch on the weather', he suggested.

'No' doubted his elder brother. 'It usually blows itself out. Anyway, it's not just me that needs to get out of here, you need to get out of here too Malcolm. Before you know it, your time will be taken up with all these menial tasks and life will have passed you by'.

'They're not *menial* Alex. I get a lot out of it', his younger brother insisted.

'What do you get out of it? Eggs?' joked his elder brother sarcastically. 'You're eighteen, for God's sake, and you haven't even had a girlfriend', he said in a serious yet condescending tone.

'Well, we can't all date the prettiest girl on the island Alex'.

'Now you're just jealous man. There are plenty women out there', exclaimed Alex. 'Just don't get aroused at the first one that floats your boat'.

'I don't get *aroused* as you call it', said Malcolm dismissively.

'No, you're right, you've probably never been aroused in your life', muttered his elder brother as he opened the croft house door.

Alex went in and sat down on the couch. He opened the newspaper. He read about the warnings of very high tides which were expected, particularly around the Orkney isles. This was due to what forecasters had named as Storm Brendan. At that moment he resolved he should leave on the ferry at two thirty in the afternoon, as he did not want to get stuck for a moment longer on the island. At least he'd get to Glasgow for around ten that night.

'I'm going to get the ferry this afternoon mother', he informed her when he returned to the small lounge. 'The weather is not getting any better'.

'That's a shame Alex. Did you see Fiona before she left this morning?' she asked.

'No. I missed her. I mean I missed the ferry', he quickly added.

'Oh, that's such a shame', his mother consoled. 'Don't you be letting that one get away now'.

'Mother!' protested Alex, accentuating his disapproval through the raised volume of his voice.

'Mark my words Alex, you'll come to regret it if you do', she stated.

'Women are the least of my worries just now', he muttered.

'If it wasn't for us *women* Alex, you wouldn't be here', his mother pointed out.

'That's not what I was meaning', he claimed.

His mother was much more astute than he often gave her credit for.

'Well, you're twenty Alex, that I'll give you. But even you will settle down one day. Just don't be looking back on what could have been. That's all I'm saying to you'.

'Thanks for the life lesson mother. I'll make a note of it for my autobiography'.

At that point his father came in from outdoors.

'Alex is leaving early. This afternoon', his mother told him.

'That's a shame Alex, but it won't be long until you're back for Easter', he suggested.

'I don't know if I want to come back Dad', stated Alex in a very matter of a fact way.

'Oh, don't be daft now Alex!' his mother exclaimed.

'No, I'm serious mother…Dad. I've had it up to here with island life. I just can't adjust to the lifestyle we have here', he informed.

'There's nothing wrong with the lifestyle here Alex', his Dad advised. 'Many people would kill to be here'.

'Aye, and many people would also be killed being here, and I'm one of them'.

'Don't be like that Alex', his mother said in her quiet and calm manner. 'I understand. You maybe feel like that now, but you'll find in time that all that happens on the mainland, is really not all that it's cracked up to be'.

'Oh mother, it is, it really is. You've just convinced yourself. What have you got? A life of domesticity, running after my Dad and Malcolm, with the odd ceilidh thrown in at the new Community Hall to look forward to'.

His mother was silent.

'Now look here Alex', said his Dad forcefully, before quieting his tone. 'You are our eldest son, and for you I have kept this croft going, as it is rightfully yours when we go'.

'But I don't want it, Dad. None of it. I never wanted this kind of lifestyle', insisted Alex.

'But it's tradition, it's a way of life, it's in our genes', insisted his father.

'It's maybe in *your* genes Dad, but I want something different from life. I want excitement, adventure, something challenging'.

'And then what Alex?' his father asked him.

'And then what what?' asked Alex.

'Now you're speaking in riddles', his father chided.

'I just don't want it. Keep it!'

And with that Alex threw open the door that separated the kitchen cum lounge with the narrow length of corridor that ran through to his bedroom. He grabbed his holdall and jacket, returning to the where his mother and father were still standing slightly aghast.

'Let me take you to the ferry', his father offered.

'No, I'll walk if you don't mind', said Alex with aggression in his voice.

'Don't leave like this Alex', said his mother with sadness in her voice. 'It needn't be like this'.

'It's not like anything mother. I'm just going to the ferry', said Alex, the tension easing a little from his voice.

'Look son, you know you always have a place here, no matter what', said his father, feeling a deep sense of sadness in his heart which his wife was also experiencing.

'I know Dad', said Alex, 'but I just can't'.

With that, he walked over to the croft house door, and shut it behind him for what he hoped would be a long time, perhaps even for the last time.

FRIENDS REUNITED

Fiona Nicolson arrived in Glasgow just after four o'clock in the afternoon. Normally she would have considered walking, but even here, in the city centre the wind was now very strong, so instead she decided to take the bus to her intended destination.

She was glad to note there was no football being held, as the bus continued its journey up Maryhill Road. Had there been so, this was the time of day the fans would all be streaming out of Firhill, if Partick Thistle, the local football team had been playing.

She hated having to negotiate the bus journey when there was football on. Usually the fans were dejected, particularly this season, and she recalled having to counsel one who was distraught as he made his way home after a match one late afternoon. She remembered thinking at the time they must have suffered a heavy loss, only to find out later in the evening, that they had in fact drawn the match. Heaven knows what he would have been like, she had thought, if they had lost it.

When she got to the parking area she looked up towards the upper floor of the complex, and was relieved to see a light in the window of the flat which her friend Mary occupied. She was on the same floor as Fiona, and had already returned some hours earlier.

Fiona opened the flat door and deposited her small case and bag on the bed situated in the corner of the room, which comprised the accommodation provided for each student. There was also a kitchenette on each floor, and a common room on the ground floor. However, people just tended to hang out in the kitchen or in their friends' rooms. Fiona was no different.

After unpacking and hanging up the clean clothing that she had returned to Glasgow with, she crossed the landing and knocked on her friend's door. It opened.

'Hi! How's you?' they greeted one another with a hug.

'How was Christmas?' asked Mary.

'Oh, Christmas was fine. It was nice to share it with my Mum and sister', she informed. 'And how was yours?'

'Yeah, great. Lots of make-up, lots of clothes and an I-pad!'
She produced it from the top of the bed upon which she had been lying.

'And how was Michael?' asked Fiona.

'Yeah, he's good. The make-up was mostly from him. In fact, we even managed an overnight at his house when his parents went away for the night'.

'Oh, serious stuff', said Fiona nudging Mary with her elbow. 'And did you?' They both laughed.

'What about you? How's Alex? He's on his final few months now?' asked Mary.

'Oh, not so good I'm afraid', said Fiona shaking her head. 'We kind of fell out yesterday, and he never came to say goodbye to me this morning, before I caught the ferry'.

'What did you fall out about?' asked Mary.

'Well, I think he's having second thoughts about going back to Raasay once he's finished his diploma for secondary teaching, once he gets this year over with. I think he feels trapped Mary'.
She looked sad.

Mary didn't really like Alex and she tried to keep back what she really wanted to say about him, for fear of hurting her friend's feelings for him. She knew they had been boy and girlfriend from the time they attended Portree High School together. She thought island life must have restricted the opportunities her friend had had to meet other boys. She had found Alex, when they first met, was always talking over her friend and was dismissive of her opinions on just about any topic you cared to mention.

'Well, maybe he's just projecting onto you his feeling of being trapped. It's unfair of him though', she consoled.

'Yeah…maybe', she said, having rejected the idea earlier during the long bus journey to Glasgow, when she had given it some very deep contemplative thought.

'Well, don't think about it just now', said her friend. 'Here have some of this!'

'What?' asked Fiona, who had perked up interest.

Mary went over to the small safe all students were provided with in their room. She punched in some digits, and the door opened to reveal some small cans of lager.
Fiona hollered in laughter.

'Well', said Mary smiling widely, 'you just never know who might get in here'.

'I've never used the small safe in my room since I got here', Fiona informed her. 'And, I never thought of using it for that!'

'Ah' said Mary passing her friend a can. 'You'd be surprised what some people put in theirs'.

'I bet …I would', laughed Fiona while half choking simultaneously, as she sipped from the can while trying to contain her laughter from overcoming her.

As the evening wore on, the two friends who had started University at the same time together, reading for their Bachelor in Education Awards, dissected and reconstructed the events of the Christmas vacation.

The conversation returned again to boyfriends and to their not infrequent misdemeanours. Fiona recounted her last conversation with Alex in some detail, and lamented what she thought might be the break-up of the relationship, with what people described on the island as her 'childhood sweetheart'.

'He really should speak to you more respectfully Fiona', her friend suggested.

'I know, but he's got a lot on his mind, with his Finals coming up. There is so much riding on them', suggested Fiona.

'Aye that maybe, but sometimes Fiona…', her friend started to speak her mind, but stopped before the effects of the drink loosened her tongue further.

'Go on, what were you going to say?' asked Fiona.

'I don't want to hurt you', said Mary keeping her comments closely guarded.

'Go on, I won't be. *I'd* say it to you whatever it is', her closest friend insisted.

'Well, I just think you have a low opinion of yourself', suggested Mary.

'What, *me*?' asked Fiona, somewhat astounded at the proposition.

'See, I knew you'd be offended', her ally confirmed.

'No, no, I'm not offended Mary. I just don't see how you can reach that conclusion'.

'Well', said Mary, 'you let him treat you like that. Sometimes if people don't think much of themselves, they'll let people treat them badly'.

'But he doesn't treat me badly', insisted Fiona.

'Well… the word doormat springs to mind', she quipped.

'I'm not a doormat!' Fiona asserted slightly bracing herself up in pseudo-sobriety.

'So, you're telling me if he arrived at your door right now, you wouldn't let him in, and probably sleep with him too?'

'Well…I…em…', said Fiona hesitantly trying to muster an intelligent response.

Several cans of lager later the conversation had moved on, and with increasing merriment and clumsiness, both realised their predicament.

'I suppose I better go back to my room and think about having a shower and going to bed for the night, or I'll never make it up in the morning'.

'And don't be letting that man into your room, or anything else for that matter!' Mary joked, as her friend departed initially the wrong way along the corridor. They both laughed.

Alex had had deep thoughts of his own once he had caught the bus after the ferry docked at Sconser. He was just glad that the ferry had sailed. He had found himself thinking through what he wanted out of life, as the bus trundled down towards the central belt from the Western Highlands.

He got to Glasgow late at night, and managed to get a taxi just outside Buchanan Street Bus Station.

When he reached his destination, he paid the taxi driver. Grabbing his holdall, he got out of the taxi where the cars were parked and looked up towards the upper floor. Soon he was climbing the stairs to the front door of the flat.

He knocked and was relieved when he heard her approach from the inside, as it was now around half past ten at night. The door opened.

'Well hello lover', said the tall slender woman. 'I was wondering when you would make it back'.

The door closed to the sound of the lock being turned from the inside.

ASSIGNATION

'I tried his mobile last night before I came to bed, but got no reply', John MacLean told his wife when they were all sitting around the table for breakfast.

'He was probably just late getting back to Glasgow and switched it off. That's all it'd be', Malcolm the younger of the two sons suggested.

'Yes maybe', said his mother. 'But I would have liked to have known that he got back safely'.

'Well dear, I'm sure we would have heard by now if he hadn't. The boat definitely sailed, though he was very lucky, as it was the last one of the day'.

'I suppose', said his wife sounding downcast.

'He'll probably phone at the weekend, just as he always does', said John trying his best to reassure her.

'I'm glad we moved that hen house into the outbuilding', said Malcolm.

'Yes indeed', snorted his father. 'It might be floating into the bay at Portree right at this moment if we hadn't. Hens and all'.

Malcolm rose from the table and left the croft house, thanking his mother on the way out for his breakfast.

'He's a good lad', his mother said wistfully to her husband.

'Aye, it's just as well' he replied.

'No, I was meaning Alex', his wife insisted.

'That maybe so', said big John, 'but I'm going to have to assign the croft over to Malcolm if he's got no interest in it'.
'Yes', said his wife sadly. 'I suppose you will'.

About one hundred and eighty miles away in a busy city, Fiona and her friend Mary were walking to their first class of the New Year. They were mid-way through the third academic year, and they were due to spend their first week back at the University campus, before spending time away on placement at educational establishments for the remainder of the term.

Some students were going overseas, but both Mary and Fiona had obtained placements within the city, enabling them both to retain their student accommodation over the academic term through to the Easter break, after which they would return again for an academic term of class-based teaching.

The wind remained very strong and had not abated much over the last 24 hours, and they were feeling it was more like an exercise session, rather than a leisurely walk, as they made their way along the busy road towards the campus.

Somewhere across the city, Alex was lying naked between the thighs of the older woman he had called upon the night before. He looked up momentarily, to see her head fling itself involuntary from side to side on the pillow, the other pillow being used to prop herself up and inserted under her buttocks. He licked again more forcefully and felt her legs shudder as she reached a climax.

She stroked his hair vigorously with her hand, moaning and lifting herself bodily off the bottom pillow, but Alex grabbed both her hands and kept kissing and licking.

'No Alex, stop!' she cried, as the intensity increased.

He eventually withdrew his head and shifted his body onto her hers, before penetrating her. And then he thrust his pelvis upwards, slowly and in a controlled manner.
Then, lifting his lover's left leg with one arm, and propping his arm on the bed, he continued to thrust slowly and deliberately.

She let out a gasp, and after several more thrusts, Alex took his arm back and positioned it alongside the other to the side of the woman's head and continued to thrust.

As the intensity continued to build more and more, she moaned and gasped, and he grunting a little, continued by keeping a steady rhythm, stopping himself from climaxing as long as he could.

She cried louder and as the bed springs creaked more and more under their collective body weight, she thrust her mouth into the muscle that arched over the top of his right shoulder, and moaned deeply into it. It took him very little time to climax after that.

He felt a certain pride in himself when she told him how good he was as he lay down beside her. Although he had got in late last night, he felt he had performed well shortly after arriving, but he felt that possibly she had not let herself go as much as she had done this morning.

'Are you coming back again tonight?' she asked, twiddling one of the few chest hairs that ran down his front. She kissed him.

'I'll see, I need to get ready for class', he informed rather coldly.

'Do come back soon Alex' she said, her voice straining a little as she lit a rather elongated cigarette. 'It's been over three weeks since we fucked each other's brains out', she added.

'You mean, since I fucked yours out', he added smugly.

'Don't be so sure', she teased.

'What do you mean?' he said slightly resenting the comment. 'Do you want me to make you squeal even louder?' he asked.

She laughed.

'No, I need to be able to walk to work in a while,' she said, stroking her own hair backwards. 'Here hold this', she said passing him a lit cigarette.

'What's this?' he asked.

'Just hash', she said calmly.

'Let me have a puff', he said inhaling deeply.

The tall woman rose out of the bed and covered her body with a silk bath robe.

'Just don't leave it three weeks this time Alex. That's all', she said taking the cannabis joint from him. She sat down beside him and stroked his naked thigh slowly.

She got up and walked through to her en-suite bathroom. She wondered if she was just another of his conquests. He was certainly handsome and muscular in appearance. Quite tall, which for her was important, as she was quite tall herself and she wanted someone taller to help her feel more secure. He came through behind her and as she looked in the mirror she saw and felt his hands come from behind cupping her breasts. She resisted pushing them down and away.

'If you want them Alex, come back tonight'.

'I can't', he said. 'I've got to catch up with my coursework'.

'Just come and study *me* then sometime this week, eh? Message me first, and I'll make it worth your while'.

She turned on the shower, and he watched as she slipped the dressing gown off her body and stepped into the shower, whilst looking back in his direction teasing him.

He turned around and went back to the bedroom and put his clothes on. Then, grabbing his holdall, he slipped out of the front door which she had left the key in the lock for him to do, as he had done on several occasions now over the last four months.

As he descended the stairs, he recalled the first time he had seen her, looking all glamorous selling make-up in the large department store. He knew then that he had to sleep with her, and on the next occasion he was in the shop, he asked her out for a drink. That had been a good move he felt, as she had relaxed in his company and invited him back for the night. He had used the opportunity to fulfill his desire, several times in fact during that first night.

He enjoyed going over regularly, as he felt she was almost as good as Helen was, but not quite. She was more passive which he didn't mind, as it let him take the initiative and test out what worked best, but he was intrigued by her suggestion that she'd make it worth his while if he returned this week. I might just take her up on that invite, he thought.

Having walked to the station he took the train to Govanhill, the area of the city where he stayed with his friends. Opening the door to the flat, he was greeted by Jerry.

'You made it, I thought you'd end up marooned on a desert island'.

'Ha!' said Alex, 'the thought of it crossed my mind too, and I came back last night just to make sure I got here in time for tomorrow'.

'So, where did you stay last night then?' his friend challenged him.

'Now wouldn't you want to know', laughed Alex, sharply moving his finger to touch his nose.

'Let me guess, was it Fiona, or …Helen?' he asked.

'Neither of them. But it was fun', he laughed.

'Bloody hell man. I don't know how you can do that', cautioned his friend.

'Jealous Jerry. That's what they call you mate', his flat mate chided in response.

'I'm not jealous. I just think women should be treated with a little respect. Well, some that is, that's all'.

'Well, I think loving them and their bodies is being respectful. In fact, Jerry, they always ask me for more, so I can't be that bad, eh?'

Alex turned and walked towards his room. He turned for one last jibe.

'Anyway mate, have you not managed to get laid yet?'

'Humph', replied Jerry and walked away.

Back on Raasay, John MacLean thought he'd try his eldest son's phone one more time. He was saddened at the thought that he would have to change his will and the assignation of the croft from Alex and into Malcolm's name.

Malcolm was eighteen, big, athletic and strong. Probably more so than his elder brother, and he took interest in the croft and in the life of the crofting community. But it was traditional to pass the assignation of the croft down to the eldest son, and this would break the mould of what had been done in the family over many generations.

Again, there was no reply, and John comforted himself in the knowledge that the son who would end up with the croft, would love and tend it, as lovingly as he had done and the generations of his forefathers before him.

During the break after the first few classes, Fiona took out her mobile phone and switched it on. She thought that possibly Alex might leave her a message. There was nothing. The words of her friend Mary from the night before, and who was busy at the counter in the cafeteria getting coffee, went through her head. She relented and sent a message:

'Hope the ferry sailed okay and you are on your road back to Glasgow. Miss you loads. xxxx'.

THE LAST SUPPER

The next day after class Fiona rushed home. Mary had been looking for her at the end of the last class, but as she couldn't find her, she presumed she maybe had an individual tutorial to attend, or something. She thought it odd however that she hadn't mentioned it when on their way to the University that morning.

Fiona called at the off-licence which was situated just around the corner from the student flats. She bought six bottles of lager and a bottle of white wine. She knew she had to manage her finances carefully, but this was a special occasion after all.

She phoned in her order to the local takeaway and quickly went up to the top floor of the student block. She entered the small kitchenette and took from the cupboard two plates, two glasses and some cutlery. Wrestling with them in her hands, along with a folder from class, and the bottles of lager and wine, she used her knee to press open the door. She, just and no more, managed to get the key into the lock with what remaining fingers she had available to her. Once in, she put everything down on the built-in desk which each student flat had as standard in their accommodation.

Drawing the curtains, she thought quickly about what she might wear for the occasion. She took a blue dress off the coat hanger, and threw off her rather mundane wear for the day. She looked in the mirror, conscious that it was quite low cut and a bit revealing. She thought about putting a stitch in it quickly to raise the neckline, but thought better of it on this occasion.

She heard the buzz of her intercom and went to answer it. Opening the door, revealed an older man who had come to deliver her food order. She thanked him, retrieving a two pound coin from the shelf in her room to offer him as a tip. She walked over and placed the food on the desk next to the alcohol.

Turning around once again, she opened the curtains to let the light in. As she looked out of the window she saw him walk across the forecourt. She waited just until the moment he was about to ring the intercom, and opened the door to surprise him.

'Now that's what I call service', Alex said aloud smiling.

'Good timing', informed Fiona. 'You must have a nose for the food,' she laughed.

'Yes, I thought it must be here, as the delivery guy just about ran me over on his bike while trying to read his mobile phone and cycle at the same time', he said sarcastically.

'Did you get back okay yesterday?' she asked politely making conversation.

'Yes, it was choppy, but I got back fine', he informed.

'Oh, I thought all the boats were cancelled yesterday', she remarked.

'So, are you ready for your placement? he asked quickly changing the conversation.

'Yes, we start on Monday. It's a bit of a hike across town involving two bus trips, but I'd rather that, than go and stay the week in Dundee, which was the alternative', she informed.

'You need to get out and about more', he suggested. She sensed one of his life lessons was forthcoming, so she rose and started to plate the carryout meal. She handed him one.

'Do you want lager or wine?' she asked.

'Lager is fine', he remarked.

She retrieved a bottle opener from underneath the desk and opened the bottle.

'Do you want a glass?' she asked.

'I'm a man', he laughed.

She plated her own meal, opened the wine bottle and poured some into a glass. She then took a seat on the floor beside the bed upon which he sat.

'Do you not want to come up and sit on the bed beside me?' he asked.
'Honest, I'm quite comfy here', she said.

He didn't mind either, for from his advantageous position he was able to look down her dress and admire her cleavage. She didn't usually wear low cut dresses, so he was pleasantly surprised and reasoned she was trying to entice him.

'What about you?' she asked.

'What about me?'

'Have you a lot of assignments this term?' she enquired.

'Yes, and exams. Where you're meant to find the time for it all, I really don't know'.

'I can never understand how some of the older students manage to do it all part-time', Fiona suggested. 'And with a family', she added quickly.

'I know', he replied. 'I think they must sleep with the tutor or something', he sneered.

'Don't be silly', she laughed.

'I'm not being silly. There's more of that goes on than people realise', he reasoned.
'This is good', he said nodding to his plate.

'Yes, they've never let us down yet', she concurred.

The conversation had a rather stilted performance to it. It had never caused them a problem before. They had grown up on the island together. There were not that many children in the local primary school on Raasay, so the difference of a year in age meant little. When they went to the High School at Portree on the main island of Skye, the Raasay children all tended to stick together too, as they would leave and come back on the same boat together. They were comfortable in each other's company. It was almost like a sixth sense. One often knew what the other was thinking, even verbalizing it on occasions before the other one had even spoken the thought aloud. But this was different, there was a certain tension that hung in the air, just as it had done a few days ago when on the island. She had noticed it creeping in to their time together over the last few months, and she wasn't too sure why. Once they had finished their meal, she decided to be assertive and try to find out why.

'Did you really mean life was hell with me around the other day Alex?' she asked.

'No, of course not. I was just stressed at everything and the thought of coming back here to all the assignments and exams over the next few months. Forget it', he said.

He sat down on the floor beside her.

'But…', she started to say, but he put his finger on her lips.

'Shhh…', he said quietly and kissed her. He then placed his hand inside her dress and started to massage her right breast. She pulled his hand away.

'What?' he exclaimed aloud.

'I thought we were just going to talk for a while', she said.

'Talk. Talk about what?' he asked angrily.

'The future. Our future Alex'.

'What future?' he demanded to know and rose to his feet.
'Look', he said, 'all you can think about is homemaking Fiona. I need space and all you seem to want to do is build a fence around me to keep me in. There's a big world out there. Why don't you go to Dundee and…', he barked.

'And what?' she asked sounding alarmed.

'Oh, go and get some experience of life Fiona!' he shouted rising to his feet, and stormed out the door, slamming it in his wake.

'Alex!' she cried after him, but it was too late. He was gone.

Mary had heard the door slam. She went to her door and looked out and she was sure she could hear her friend sobbing behind her flat door.

Fiona was behind the door, and was indeed crying while trying to wrestle the top off her inhaler. She had been diagnosed a year ago with adult asthma, which seemed to be triggered as much by anxiety, as by anything else environmental.

Do I go over and knock, or not? Mary asked herself, but her legs had already answered the question having walked across the landing to her friend's door. She knocked quietly.

'Fiona', she said gently. 'It's me, Mary'.

The door opened and Fiona had her face down as she let her friend in to the flat. Mary gave her a hug and Fiona just broke her heart.

He wasn't too perturbed. He hadn't really been into it, what with the little rendezvous and meals indoors together. He walked towards the bus stop and caught a bus down into the city centre. He decided against going back to Govanhill for the moment. Taking his mobile phone from his jacket pocket, he started messaging on it.

When he got near Central Station, he got off the bus. As he walked around the corner to a large wine bar, he saw an older man with a walking aid who tried to stop him and ask him something, but he walked on dismissively, brushing past him. As he looked back in his direction, he saw the older man overbalance and fall off the kerb off the pavement, and into the road. He stopped for a moment and thought about whether or not he should help him. But deciding it was busy enough and that someone else would probably stop to assist him, he carried on towards his destination.

As he walked on, he thought how Glasgow was getting more chic each time that he came back to it. Wine bar or not, he ordered himself a lager. He took a drink from the bottle while standing at the bar and saw on the television all the damage that the recent storm had caused across the country. He was engrossed in the news, when he felt someone tap on his shoulder.

He turned around and she kissed him thrusting her tongue into his mouth, causing him to gasp momentarily. She was always forthcoming. He liked that in a woman, forthcoming and not shy to take the initiative.

'So, you're back', she said with a smile coming across her face.

'Yes, I got back a few nights ago', he informed her.

'So why has it taken you a few nights to get in touch with me? Did the man from Skye lose his trousers or something?' she mocked, alluding to the words of a well- known Scottish song.

He hated when she called him that, but he was happy enough to disregard it on this occasion, as he was pleased to see her. She was about medium height for a woman, blonde haired, blue eyed, sex on legs.

'Let's grab a table', she said pointing to the side of the room where a couple had just vacated one.
'Can you bring me a glass of Chardonnay?' she asked turning to the barman, though it sounded much more like an instruction. She had an assertive manner about her.

The barman duly obeyed and the couple sat down at the table, smiling across it at one another.

'So, are you going to Southside or are you coming to mine?' she asked him invitingly, and taking a foot from one of her heeled shoes, she rested it on his crotch. The red painted toenails probed until he flinched.

'I think you already know the answer to that one', he said.

She withdrew her foot and sensuously drank from her wine glass looking at him over the rim of it as she did so. He was besotted by her and she definitely wanted him as much as he wanted her tonight. He drank up and she just as quickly finished hers. In some sort of symbolic ritual, she took the keys out of her purse and handed them to him.

They didn't have far to walk to reach her flat in the centre of town. He followed her up the stairwell. She stopped midway, remembering he had the keys. She stood on the step above him and gently pressed her knee between his legs. She forcefully kissed him and took the keys from his hand.

When they finally got through the door of the flat, she led him by the hand straight through to the bedroom. They stripped one another quite frantically, and as he went to kiss her as she lay on the bed, she pushed him over and sat on top of him pressing her tongue between his lips and into each cheek, and as she did so she squeezed his buttock hard.

He felt very aroused and he enjoyed the moment.

Then she grabbed his hands and forcibly pushed them above his head, reaching across and into a drawer of a small sideboard that sat beside the bed. She pulled out a tie and tied his wrists loosely together with the silken fabric.
She then worked her way down his body with her lips, first the contours of his chest and then down towards his genitalia. Realising he was aroused, she straddled him and being sure he was inside, started to thrust gently at first and then repeatedly.

He hooked his tied hands over her head, then her shoulders, with a view to turning her over on the bed, so that he was now the one that was on top. But before he could do so she stopped momentarily, fully in control of the situation. She ducked out from under his conjoined hands and tied the loop of the tie that held them loosely together, even tighter. Then she moved Alex's hands over the bed knob at the side of the headboard and continued.

She thrust repeatedly, over and over again, until his body gyrated and he grunted for her to stop. She continued a little longer until she was sure she was satisfied, and that he really could take no more.

Fiona was still tearful, but much to Mary's relief had stopped sobbing by now. They both sat drinking the lager that was left over from the not so romantic dinner.

'You've got to make a stand Fiona', her good friend advised her again. 'Otherwise, he'll think he can just snap his fingers and good auld Fiona will come running back. You just don't think you're good enough, that's it, isn't it?'

'Good enough for what exactly?' quizzed Fiona.

'Good enough to be respected for the beautiful woman you are Fiona'.

Mary was aware that her friend had lost her father just over a year ago, and that it had had a massive impact on her. The chirpy, sprightly, and really quite cheeky friend that she had met at the start of their first year together at teacher training, had become self-doubting and anxious, and yes even sometimes an insular individual.

'I hate to see anyone treat you this way Fiona. I'm sorry, hate me for saying it if you want, but he's an *absolute bastard* to you'.

Fiona stopped snivelling. She was taken aback momentarily at her friend's bluntness. She gulped and then she laughed, and then laughed even more as if she had lost control of herself. Mary could not but help join in as Fiona's laugh was infectious, but she wasn't absolutely sure what it was exactly she was laughing at. But she was just glad her friend was no longer crying.

THE MAN WITH NO NAME

It had been several years now since the island had had a resident nurse in place and now there would be several of them.

Janice felt both excited and uneasy when she heard she had been successful at interview and that she was to start just a few weeks after the other three had taken up post. She had come across from Inverness the day before she was due to start and had found the terraced property in the main village in Inverarish easily. In fact, it really was the only place on the island that you could describe nowadays as being the main village.

The small row of terraced cottages, originally known as Inverarish Houses, had been built just before the outset of the First World War, and were used during the Great War to house the German prisoners. The prisoners were to be used to help mine iron ore, from the mine on the island.

She found the road leading up from the pier quite narrow. She had been used to the narrow roads around Inverness, with several being single track, but the island's roads were even narrower than that.

Janice was still very young and had only graduated recently. They had admired her enthusiasm at the interview, and although not so certain about her level of experience, the Nursing Manager for the area had felt that given the other three part time appointments were older, more mature, and more experienced, she would fit in well as one of a team of four and probably learn greatly from her older colleagues.

But the first trip to Mrs. MacKay at south Oscaig had not gone so well. She had called on the elderly lady and re-dressed her leg, but on the road back towards Inverarish, she had accidentally driven into a ditch close to where a Pictish stone lay near to the roadside.

Her mobile signal was poor, and other than try to phone the other nurse who was on duty, she really was not too sure what to do given her predicament. There was no garage or A.A. service that she was aware of on the island. They had been reminded, on at least one day a fortnight, to ensure they took their cars which were leased from the N.H.S. over to Skye, to fill them with petrol.

She stood there looking at the wheels that were grounded and which she couldn't get out of the ditch. She had tried to see if one of the wheels could gain traction, but she had probably only made it worse, as the side of the ditch where she had tried to extract the vehicle from, was mud.

But as fate would have it, she was not long on her own, because a tractor approached coming from the north down towards the big house. A man about her own age, perhaps a little younger, stopped and got out of the driver's cab.

'Can I help you?' the young man asked. He was quite tall and muscular. In fact, she thought he was quite attractive for a farmer.

'Yes, I have gone into the ditch, and I just can't get the car out of it. Do you know if there is a garage, or the A.A. or R.A.C. or someone I can call about here to get me out of it?' she asked.

'No, there's none of these things here', he informed.

'So, what are you meant to do if you get stuck?' she asked, a little frustrated.

'Oh, we just get by', he responded a little too glibly for her liking.

'Well, that's not much use if you don't know someone who can help', she retorted, more than a little unamused at what she felt was an unhelpful response to the serious predicament she found herself in.

'Any of us would help', he responded, thinking it was pretty obvious.

'Oh, I see…and can you?' she asked, aware that she maybe had pre-judged the young man who stood talking with her.

'Of course, that's why I drove here when I saw you', he said.

'Oh, I see', she replied reddening a little in her face. 'Do you think it's badly damaged?' she asked bending over to talk with him, as he had stooped over to look at the ditched wheels.

'I really won't know until we take it out, but it looks pretty okay to me from this angle. Just a lot of mud on the bumper and wheel arches, but that's all', he informed.

Going over to the tractor he took out a rope and hooked it over a hook at the front of his tractor, and similarly attached it to the towing eye on the rear of her vehicle. He jumped in his cab, reversed the tractor, and moments later the little car popped up and sat on the road. He jumped out, loosened the ropes and looked under her car.

'I honestly think it looks fine. If you drive it a few yards forward and backwards we'll be able to tell', he suggested.

She climbed in the driver's seat and drove a little down the road, before reversing ever so slowly back towards the cab. At first, she was in dread as she heard a clunking sound, but then it sounded normal, once a small clump of mud had dislodged itself from under the wheel arch and which bounded along the road.

'Well?' he asked inquisitively.

'Yes, thanks', she replied very pleased it had not done any damage. 'Is there anything I can do to thank you?' she asked politely.

'No honest, I'm glad I could help. You'll be busy with all your patients', he reasoned aloud.

'How did you know that' she asked, surprised he knew she was a Community Nurse given she had only been on the island a few days.

'Well', he laughed. 'Asides from the uniform…', he added smiling.

She laughed thinking herself to be a bit stupid.

'But seriously', he quickly added sensing her embarrassment, 'they say everyone round here knows how much the other person has in their electric meter'.

'And how much do I have in mine?' she asked, a bit taken aback at the suggestion.

'It's just an expression', he said, realising she had taken him literally.

'Oh', she said, feeling even more silly now.

'Tell you what', he suggested. 'Would you come out for a drink tonight?'

'No', she said. He looked disappointed. 'I'm on-call tonight…but I can this weekend if you'd like. Maybe on Saturday?'

His head shot up.

'Yes, great', he said.

'What time shall we meet?' she asked.

'Is seven o'clock okay?' he asked.

'Seven is fine', she said, and with that he jumped in the cab of his tractor. He started up the engine and was about to move away, when he saw her waving to her. He opened the cab door.

She shouted towards him.

'Where?'

'Oh, there only is Raasay House', he said. 'I'll meet you inside at seven'.

And with that he drove off, leaving her a little bemused that she hadn't even asked his name.
He better turn up, she thought, because if he doesn't I'm going to look really stupid sitting there, and if anyone asks who I'm waiting for, I can hardly tell them that I don't even know his name.

REIMAGINING THE FUTURE

'How did you get on in Inverness?' Christina MacLean asked her husband, when he came through the door that evening.

'Oh fine', said big John in a resigned tone of voice, 'I did what I had to do'.

'Maybe we should have spoken to him first again, before we signed it over', his wife suggested. 'It would have given him time to cool off, to maybe change his mind'.

'I don't think so', her husband affirmed. 'I tried to phone him twice this week, but he can't even be bothered to get back to me'.

The couple sat down to dinner.

'Where's Malcolm?' he asked, looking around the room as if he had somehow missed the presence of his younger son.

'Ah, he's gone to Portree and will be back off a later boat', smiled his wife.

'What are you grinning at?' asked John. 'Has something broken or something?'

'No', said his wife, 'but don't tell him I told you so'.

'Told me what?' he asked rather bemused at the lack of information.

'He's got a date!' she exclaimed.

'Well, I'll be damned', her husband retorted. 'Whoever can it be?'

'Well', whispered his wife.

'What are you whispering for?' John asked laughing.

'In case someone hears', she advised.

'There's no-one going to hear us sitting here in the house', he laughed. 'These walls are as impenetrable as Fort Knox'.

'It's a young woman called Janice', she informed.

'Janice…I don't think I know anyone on the island with that name', he replied giving it some deep thought.

'No, she's new. She's one of the new nurses'.

'Oh, about time too' said John emphatically.

'He's still young yet John', she smiled.

'No, I mean it's about time that they employed a nurse here. How long have we gone without one? Inverness doesn't care about what goes on outside Inverness', he stated just as emphatically as he has done in his initial proposition.

'Well now there are four of them', his wife continued, 'and the youngest is a young lady called Janice. She attends to Jeannie's leg ulcer each day'.

'And how do you know all this?' asked her husband.

'Because I noticed yesterday morning, he was watching with great interest the comings and goings of the nurse's car. So, I asked him outright'.

'What did you say?'

'I said to him what are you seeing there Malcolm? And he came right out and said it. He told me he was going on a date with the nurse in the car tomorrow night'.

'Well, I'll be damned', said her husband eating a potato whilst shaking his head.

'But that's not all. I even paid Jeannie a visit later on yesterday afternoon, and she told me she is a very nice lass'.

'And he's a nice laddie too', suggested her husband. 'Takes after his father'.

'And modest too', quipped Christina.

Back in Glasgow, Mary was waiting for her friend Fiona to arrive home from her placement.

'So how was week one then?'

'It was good, except for one boy today who bit a girl in the playground', informed Fiona.

'Bloody hell…and what did you do?' Mary asked.

'I have to be honest Mary; I struggled a bit with it. I separated them and then took the boy aside and told him to go over to the Headteacher's room. And then I spent the next five minutes consoling the girl he had bitten'.

'Animal!' retorted Mary. 'But it sounds like you did all the correct things Fiona'.

'I did, I know. But when Mr. McGillivray came to ask me why the boy was sitting on the chair outside his room, I went to explain it all and kept losing my breath'.

'Your asthma?'

'Yes, my bloody asthma. I felt like a fool, fumbling around for my inhaler, between each sentence'.

'But you dealt with it correctly', her friend consoled.

'Yes, and he did say that. But I felt foolish gasping away as if I was some sort of anxious child just out of school, who didn't know what she was doing'.

'But you did Mary. You can't help having asthma'.

'It'll be the death of me!' responded Fiona angry with herself.

'Don't say that; at least it's the weekend now'.

'Yes', agreed Fiona, half wondering if she'd hear from Alex.

But Saturday night came without a text, or call.

Instead, Alex was undressing his tall slender friend, pinning her against her apartment wall. She had promised if he visited again, she would make it worth his while. And she did. She was a bit annoyed at first when he had phoned, as it had been about a fortnight since she had suggested he might visit her, and he had agreed to come at six and it had now touched seven. But she had greeted him at her door, wearing no more than a bikini, which revealed more than anything it covered.

He had removed the top and untied the side of the bikini bottom, which released it from her body and it fell to the floor. She undid his trousers as he kissed her neck frantically, and then he pushed her shoulders against the wall. Remaining standing, and because of her height, he positioned his knees between her thighs and thrust repeatedly as she hooked her arms under his shoulders.

Malcolm rose from the table when Janice entered the bar at Raasay House on the stroke of seven. He was wearing a suit
He rose to remove the chair from under the table for Janice.

'I'm glad you're here', she said to him quietly.

'Why wouldn't I be?' he asked smiling at her opening statement.

'Because I don't even know your name, and I would have appeared a bit stupid sitting here if you hadn't turned up'.

'Eh…Malcolm', he informed, and then said 'Janice?'

She had never told him her name either, so she was a little taken aback.

'So how do you know *my* name?' she asked. But she answered the question simultaneously with the same response he gave,

' …*they say everyone round here knows how much the other person has in their electric meter*'.

They both laughed aloud together.

Fiona was sitting in her room getting ready to meet up with Mary and her boyfriend. She felt like she was playing gooseberry, but she didn't want to sit there on a Saturday night, wondering whether or not to phone Alex. He was, after all, as she knew, very busy with the forthcoming exams.

As Alex's fingers caressed and examined the body of his tall slender lover, he felt her grip him tighter and he knew he was about to make her climax. It had all been very quick and passionate, so he spent a little more time kissing her neck and down into her breasts, before thrusting more vigorously once again. She squeezed him tight towards her as he thrust, causing her to gasp louder and louder.

Malcolm asked his new found friend what she would like to drink.
One of the benefits of island life was that most things were within walking distance, so you didn't need to drive everywhere. Unless of course you lived in Arnish, or somewhere in the north of the island.

Janice took a sip of her wine, and they talked about their backgrounds. She was quite concerned at the news of a virus that was spreading to other parts of the world, which had originated in China and was now in Europe.

'It is only a matter of time', she had informed, 'until it comes here'.

'What, to Scotland?' he asked.

'Yes, it really could be quite serious'.

Back in Glasgow, Fiona was now in the Student's Union with her friend Mary, and her boyfriend Michael. They sat at a table and mumbled agreeable comments about the band that had been playing.

'I'm sure they'll make it big', Michael asserted, but Mary was less committal.

'What do you think Fiona?' she asked.

'Eh…I think…', she began, but was interrupted mid-sentence by one of the older male students who came over to speak with her.

'Do you want to dance?' he asked.

'Eh no, I…', she responded.

'A drink?' He was not giving up.

'No, thanks', she said, 'I've got one, and I'm just really here for a quiet night'.

'Okay, please yourself', he smiled and walked off.

'Why did you say that?' asked Mary a little taken aback at her friend's rebuttal of this good-looking guy's advances.

'I …'

'Go on', said Mary pushing her.

'If you must know, I don't want to be disloyal'.

'Oh, for fuck's sake Fiona. Do you really think for a moment that Alex is sitting there on a Saturday night, with his head in his books?'

Alex lay there on the floor, with his head on her breasts. She stroked his hair.

'You still got some hash?' he asked.

'Yes, but you will have to earn it first', she teased.

Malcolm and Janice got on well. They sat and talked after they had eaten, and for a first date they had found it relatively easy to talk to one another. As they finished their drinks, Malcolm took her jacket from her chair and opened it for Janice to put her arms into.

'Can I walk you home?' he asked.

It was only a five minute walk down the hill and along to Inverarish, and despite the unsettled weather, it was quite a pleasant night.

'Oh, go on then', she laughed.

As they walked Malcolm told her about the battle of Churchton Bay.

'You certainly know your history Malcolm MacLean', she said.

She kissed him gently on the cheek. He hadn't expected that and he was glad it was dark, as he felt his face reddening.

Alex thrust his tongue into his lover's cheek, seeking out every sensitive part of her body. And as he moved his hands, he felt her gasp that familiar gasp again, and again, the more he moved them. And then her body quivered, and as she tried to move his hand away, he maintained his position, and enjoyed watching her cry out loudly and uncontrollably in ecstasy.

'What do you say Michael?' Mary asked, trying to goad her boyfriend into agreeing with her. But she didn't have to try too hard.

'Yes, if your boyfriend wants to study, or do other things, it doesn't mean you can't go out and enjoy yourself'.

'I know, but you know what it's like. If I say yes, then it just raises expectations'.

'And what of it, Fiona?' asked Mary accusingly. 'I don't know if Alex has had other girlfriends or not, but maybe if he realised he can't just snap his fingers and you will be at his beck and call, he might start to treat you better'.

'But we have planned our future', Fiona protested.

'Well maybe you need to reimagine your future then', asserted Mary, slightly regretting being so forthright in her opinion.

Janice said goodnight to her date. He had not asked to come in, or make any suggestive comments. In fact, he had been a pleasant companion for the night, and had said goodnight at her front door.
She hadn't really imagined meeting anyone on Raasay, given its population size, and although she never knew what life might bring, she was already wondering just what the future might bring.

Alex lay there feeling quite pleased with himself. He thought to himself when he next met with Helen, he might tie her to the bed post this time, and do what he had just done to the woman he had had tonight. He was reimagining who would be the dominant one in bed this time, when his lover for this night returned with the hash.

CRISIS MANAGEMENT

The next morning, Malcolm's mother enquired gently as to how her younger son's first date had gone. She was mindful that when compared to his elder brother, he lacked the confidence which he exhibited, so she hoped it had gone well for him.

'Yes, a good night was had by all', he informed.

'Oh, that's lovely dear', she responded encouragingly and had a happy smile to herself.

Janice's colleagues had also enquired on the Monday of their youngest member of the staff team how it had gone. It was not hard to do your homework on Raasay, as you could be sure people would know of the event, and would be only too willing to express an opinion on a person's character and impart a little life history to any willing listener.

'I think it went well', she told Margaret her colleague for the day's rounds.

'I hear he is a nice lad', Margaret informed. 'Not like his brother'.

'Oh, he's got a brother?' said Janice a little surprised. When she asked, she was conscious she had probably talked about herself maybe too much, and not asked enough about him.

'Yes, he's the boyfriend of one of the girls in the village here. They're both at University, but they say he's not very nice to her'.

'What do you mean?' asked Janice, 'not very nice'.

'Well', whispered Margaret, 'you never heard this from me mind you'.

'No, no', reassured Janice.

'Well, they say he is a bit of a ladies' man'.

'Is he good looking?' she asked.

'I think so', Margaret informed. 'I only saw him once when I was visiting Mrs. MacKay, close to where they stay at Oscaig. Too young for me and how can I put it politely? Well, he thinks he's God's gift, as they say'.

'Oh', said Janice thoughtfully, and then thinking aloud mumbled, 'I wonder if it has rubbed off on Malcolm?'

'I don't think so from what I hear dear', Margaret reassured. 'How did you find him?'

'He was nice, the perfect gentleman as they say', informed Janice.

'Yes, I think that corresponds to how people find him, or certainly talk of him in that way', she added.

'Now I was going to take all the patients beyond the Big House today, and you could do south?' Margaret suggested.

'Oh, why's that?' asked Janice.

'Well, there's much more distance to cover, and it'd would ensure you are able to get back for the emergency meeting at the surgery at one o'clock today'.

'Oh, I'll be fine', suggested Janice, 'I'd rather keep the north side if you don't mind'.

'Okay then', Margaret agreed trying to keep a straight face as her younger colleague picked up her equipment.

Janice smiled to herself as she walked to her car with her case of utensils in hand.

As she drove by the big house where she had gone for dinner, she was mindful to go easy at the bend. It would be embarrassing, she thought, if she drove the car into the ditch again.

Malcolm was out fixing a fence that adjoined a cattle grid by the roadside that morning. He had been thinking of what excuse he could make to go and see Janice again. Maybe if he accidentally cut himself with the broken spar which had come away from the post, then he could visit and ask her if she might dress it for him. But he thought that was both a transparent and pathetic excuse. Why do I need an excuse he thought, why don't I just go to her door and ask her out again? This was now the second day and she might think he wasn't interested in her.

Mrs. MacKay's leg was improving, Janice noted.

'Aye, maybe in another week or two it all be healed', she suggested to her elderly patient.

'That's good', she said, adjusting her hearing aids which let out a high-pitched whine.

'Now tell me dear, how did your big date go on Saturday night?' she asked.

'Goodness me Mrs. MacKay', said Janice blushing, 'you really can't keep a secret around here'.

'Oh, don't be like that', the older woman laughed, 'we just want the best for you'.

'Well…it went well, I think', she offered by way of information.

'Aye, he's a nice lad is that Malcolm. You could do much worse than him. You know, when this ailment of mine started and I was laid up, he came here for the first month every day and cleaned and set my fire for me until I could get about a bit better and do it myself'.

'That was nice of him', said Janice.

'Yes, he's quiet, but I think that is because he has been a bit overshadowed by his older brother, Alex'.

'Yes, I heard he had an older brother'.

'Of course you have my dear. It's strange you know'.

'What's strange?' Janice asked.

'It's strange how children in the same family can sometimes turn out so different'.

'And what's so different about them?' the young nurse asked.

'Well', replied the elder, 'let's just say if Alex was made of chocolate he'd eat himself'.

They laughed.

'But they say he is good looking?' Janice suggested.

'Yes, I suppose he is', the older lady said, 'but take my advice. There is much more to be said for a kind heart than good looks. Look at me, my skin is like an old prune!'

They both laughed again.

'Not at all Mrs. MacKay'.

'Yes my dear, it's true even though I say it myself. I dare say Malcolm's brother is a good looker, as they say, and I think anyone who is just after a good time would be quite happy with that. But others want more out of life', she reasoned, imparting her wisdom like some wise old owl.

The words went around Janice's head as she rounded the corner, nearly knocking her first date over on the roadside. She stopped and lowered her window to apologise.

'I missed you!' she gasped.

'That's very kind of you to say that Janice', he replied.

'No, no, not in that way', she said, a little too sternly half castigating herself and him too for not understanding her meaning.

'Oh, I see', he said a little dejected.

'No, no, I don't mean it in that way', she tried to excuse her turn of phrase but probably only managed to exacerbate the situation further.

'It's okay', he said calmly. 'I'm okay with saying I missed you'.

'What?' she said taken aback at the turn of the conversation.

'I missed you. I've been standing here all morning thinking of an excuse to go and see you, like cutting my hand or something', he said looking up at her through the car window.

'Oh', she laughed. 'You don't need an excuse Malcolm. I'm off on Wednesday. We could do something then if you'd like?'

'Sure. Brilliant. I could call round…say nine in the morning?' he suggested.

'A woman needs her beauty sleep', she responded, 'how about ten?'

'I'll see you about ten then', he agreed laughing.

As she drove off, he smiled to himself and thought about just how beautiful she actually was, but also at how bad a driver she was too.

Instead of going home, Janice drove up to the surgery near the Primary School for the meeting of health professionals.

As she left the meeting later that afternoon, she felt quite sombre at the crisis that could potentially in time, come to threaten the island's way of life.

HOMECOMING

Despite being a leap year, as the shortest month, February seemed to come and go too quickly.

Fiona and Mary were in the middle of their placements at Primary schools in Glasgow. Malcolm and Janice had gone on their second date, and several more thereafter. Romance was blossoming and they had even taken the daunting step of going round to his parents for dinner one evening in response to his mother's invitation, which had passed off remarkably well. Both Malcolm's parents were taken with the beautiful Janice, as he had described her to himself on the day that she had nearly run him over.

The croft was in good shape and they were beginning to get the early potatoes ready for planting in the field over the next few weeks. There was also the prospect that the distillery might be wanting a further crop of barley this year. John was pleased that his youngest son, was taking more of an interest in the business side of crofting. In fact, he had arranged the purchase, delivery and helped in the instillation of the three camping pods. He hoped that would provide an additional income over the summer months, as asides from the big house and a few self-catering rentals, there was little accommodation on the island for tourists.

Even Alex had managed to apply himself a little more to preparatory study for his forthcoming exams. He knew he still had his needs to be met, but he could do that with one simple text or just one call.

So, it was with some surprise that everyone was rocked by suggestions in the papers and on the news, early the following month, that the schools, colleges and universities might have to close. The Government was adamant that this would not be the case, and the risks of the virus spreading across the country were low.

As the first few weeks of the month passed, events moved rapidly, and it became clear that what was not going to happen was about to happen. Janice was quite clear on the likelihood of the coronavirus spreading throughout the country, and the World Health Organisation had just declared it a global pandemic.

Shortly thereafter Fiona and Mary were told that the University would be closing at the beginning of the new week, and the schools had already decided to close, to minimize the risk of the virus spreading in the community. They were advised to return home in the next few days.

Alex was concerned that his exams would be affected, but the University had similarly advised his year that they should return home, and that any exams to be completed in his final year could be taken on-line.

His flat mates had all but abandoned the flat, and he decided that rather than go home to Raasay, which he really did not want to do, that he would stay put.

Despite several calls from both parents, and from Fiona, which he ignored, he used the first few days of respite from University to indulge his passions. But as the week progressed, he found his female friends were no longer as keen to see him. Alex was also mindful that he had little money left for food, and his flat mates had left little when they left.

As he sat there that night, he thought he had found some chocolate that one of them had left in one of the kitchen drawers, but after taking the first bite he spat it out in disgust. Turning over the wrapper to see what it was, he found it was carob, a poor substitute. Obviously it was Jerry's, and had formed part of his vegan health food diet, which he insisted kept him fit – though not quite in the way that others would use the term. All he knew about carob was that it grew in pods, and he resolved at that moment to return to Raasay, to prepare for his exams. But that night he tossed and turned, as he could not bring himself to stay in that claustrophobic house.

The next morning, he caught the bus from Buchanan Street station at around ten o'clock. The driver had told him that he had done well to get it at all, as they were talking about bringing in a more restricted timetable, which may not have connected with the ferry at Sconser.

The bus journey was long and arduous as it always was, and as he sat there staring out the window, bored and fearing the monotony of island life, he started to overhear and listen in to a telephone conversation a woman passenger was having.
She was clearly making arrangements with her boyfriend or fiancée, to collect her stuff from his house in Fort William. It was plain for all to hear, that they had separated, and she was telling him what he should take and what she was planning to have from their shared house.

He thought there was a sort of sad aspect to it all. But then again, he reasoned maybe like Fiona, she wasn't that interested in doing anything other than making home. He decided when he got back to the island, to call on her and maybe give her another shot. Maybe he owed her one last chance, he thought. She certainly was not as bubbly as she used to be, before her Dad died the previous year.

As he waited for the ferry to come into the harbour, he finally saw it emerge with the island's highest peak, Duncaan, serving as a backdrop.
His old schoolfriend, Duncan, who was just as big as the hill itself, was working as the crew hand. He seemed to be growing bigger with each journey, and Alex thought he was a far cry from the schoolboy athlete, who managed to outpace everyone at cross country racing throughout the High School years. What he lacked in academic ability at school, he had certainly made up for it in athleticism.

'Aye, you're lucky to get this one', Duncan told him.

'The bus driver was saying the same', Alex informed. 'He was….'.

The walkie talkie from the bridge interrupted his friend.

'I'll catch up with you before you get off, or maybe later at the Big House?' his friend suggested.

Alex didn't ask what time, as he knew when the ferry docked for the night, whatever night it was, his friend could be found at Raasay House sampling their range of whiskies.

79

On the ferry, he saw Alan Kennedy, who lived in Glame, just a little further up the road from Oscaig where his parents lived. He offered him a lift, but it was a nice enough night, and he thought it would also give him time to think through what he was going to say to his parents. He was conscious he was going to have to depend on them over the next few weeks until the University re-opened, if it in fact re-opened, and he had not exactly left them on amicable terms.

That was why as he reached the cattle grid, he was more than surprised to meet his father walking hurriedly down the road towards him.
His father greeted him with open arms.

'Why didn't you tell me you were coming home Alex, and I would have come to the pier and picked you up?'

'Ever since the pier moved to the big house Dad, it's really cut the walk in half. Anyway, I thought you'd be busy. How did you know I was here?' Alex asked.

'Old Alan Kennedy passed me at the roadside when I was putting the jam your mother makes in the roadside box, and he stopped and told me you were coming off the ferry. He said he felt bad as you wouldn't take a lift from him'.

'Aye, that's right enough. I just wanted to give a bit of thought of how I might study in peace when I'm at home', Alex informed.

'Right enough', said his father, 'it is a bit cramped for you coming to think of it'.

There was a short period of silence and then his father's face lit up.

'By jove I've got it!' he exclaimed.

'Got what?' asked Alex intrigued.

'Why don't you take one of the new glamping pods, down on the potato field. You can turn it into an office', his father suggested.

'What… the pig pods?' his son asked with a slight tone of disgust in his voice.

'Yes', said his father enthusiastically, 'take one of the pig pods or whatever you want to call it'.

As they approached the small croft house, Alex took one look and turned to his father.

'Yes, I think I will take it and turn it into a bedroom cum office, if you don't mind'.

'No son, it's yours', his father assured him.

Sunday passed off without much happening, as most Sundays did on Raasay, as Alex perceived it. Instead, he got an old camp bed out the barn and walked down to the pod with it. His father also had an old, albeit rather battered table, which he commandeered from beside his workbench and took down to the pod. He spent the Sunday night in the cramped bedroom with Malcolm, whom he found to be a bit distant, on finding his brother had returned unexpectedly.

After their evening meal on the Monday, they all watched the television and listened to the Prime Minister announcing a lockdown for the next three weeks.

'Aye', said John MacLean shaking his head, 'they say the distillery has also decided to shut down production over the next few weeks too. Whatever is the world coming to?'

'Looks like you got back just in time dear', said his mother to her eldest son. 'You don't have to sleep down there, all on your own you know', she added.

'I know mother', said Alex, 'but I need my own space'.

And the conversation was left at that.

Christina MacLean confided in her husband later that night.

'It is so nice to have him home', she said.

But as her younger son, Malcolm, lay in his bed awake in the room next door, he was not quite so sure of that.

KNOCKDOWN

Although the clocks were not due to be changed until the next weekend, Alex awoke with the light coming through the glazed door panels of his pod.

He rose from the creaky camp bed, stretched, and opened wide the doors of his temporary abode.

The sun had not quite risen yet, though the birds were vocal, and it felt like it was just himself and no-one else in the world, as he looked out towards Portree bay on Skye.

On the ground in neat little rows, he could see the first potato shoots poking through the ground and into the white mesh his brother used to protect them from frost. He heard he had managed to acquire for himself a girlfriend, and he hoped he was as diligent in attending to her needs as he was his potatoes. He smiled to himself and went back indoors.

Although it was a pod, and pods were for pigs, as he had described it, it was remarkably comfortable, water tight and peaceful. He would have to walk to the croft house to wash and take a flask of coffee back with him to the pod, but at least he had managed to carve out his own private space, whilst having all the creature comforts of home round about him.

Technically he should not be visiting another household, if you listened to what the Prime Minister had said, but as it was the same household, Alex felt it was legitimate. He also felt it was legitimate to walk down to Raasay stores, and although he shouldn't call on Fiona, as she was in a different household, he felt he owed her one final chance.

After he washed and shaved, and had the cooked breakfast that his mother had prepared for him, Alex dropped the flask off at the pod and walked towards the main village.

'I need to stock up on a few essentials', he assured the shopkeeper of the community owned store, before leaving with a bag stuffed full of bread, biscuits and chocolate. He also added some cigarettes. Not that he smoked much, but he had found since smoking the hashish that one of his girlfriends had a regular supply of, he had developed a taste for the odd cigarette.

'The ferry is now going to be essential travel only too', the shopkeeper informed him, but he was thinking through in his head how best to entice Fiona, that he simply grunted some brief response of acknowledgment.

He reached Fiona's house and knocked on the wooden door.

Her mother came to the door, took one look at him, and said,

'You shouldn't be here Alex. We are meant to be social distancing'.

Then she turned and shouted up the stairs,

'Fiona, that's Alex for you'.

As always there would be no keeping that secret, he thought to himself in derision.

Fiona appeared in the doorway once her mother turned around and had gone back inside to attend to whatever it was she had been doing beforehand.

'Oh', she said in a matter of a fact way. 'What do you want Alex? I haven't heard from you in weeks Alex, why now?'

'Eh, my phone broke, sorry about that', he advised her.

'And you didn't know where I stay?' she shot back at him.

'Look Fiona', he said, 'I know things didn't quite go as planned last time we got together, but I get that you've have been quite tense recently and I just thought I better give you some space'.

'Alex Maclean!' she exclaimed. 'That's rubbish and you know it. If you thought there was a chance of sex, you would have been straight at the door the very next morning'.

'Well', he smiled, knowing she had revealed great precision in her understanding of him, 'I'm happy to give you another chance'.

'Give *me* another chance', she spluttered. 'I'm not your doormat Alex!' she hollered.

'Well please yourself', he said. 'If you want to live in your prisoner of war house, in your prisoner of war lifestyle, that's up to you Fiona. I want something more out of life'.

She slammed the door in his face.

That didn't go down too well, he mused to himself as he walked back towards Oscaig. He had just got close to the entrance to the footpath to Temptation Hill, when a Ford Fiesta rounded the corner at speed. He stood aside, but the driver had to slow right down to safely pass him. It was a woman driver. He waved in acknowledgment, and probably still not too used to island ways, she stopped and lowered her window.

'Can I help you?' she asked.

'No, not unless you want to give me a lift back to my house', he responded.

'Sorry…I thought you were waving for me to stop', she informed. 'Normally I would offer you a lift', she added, 'but I'm afraid with the pandemic it would not be wise. I'm presuming you're taking your daily exercise'.

Alex held up his shopping bag.

'Essential shopping *actually*', he replied sarcastically, taking no life lesson from some woman who looked younger than him.
'And who are you exactly?' he asked, resentful at the intrusion into his movements.

'I'm Janice', she informed, 'one of the community nurses'.

'Well Janice', he quipped, 'I thought maybe you were one of the community policemen'.

'I didn't know we had any', she replied.

'We don't', he snorted, 'and we don't need any now thanks'.
And with that he walked off.

As she drove off, she was a little shaken by the man who did not look much older than herself.

'That leg is definitely much better now', she told her elder patient, Mrs. MacKay.

'You're not quite yourself this morning', the older woman suggested, and Janice then recounted the story of her journey that morning.

'That'll be the brother I told you about. He came home yesterday', she informed the young nurse.

'What Alex?' she queried.

'Yes, he probably thought he was beyond challenge, particularly coming from a woman', explained Mrs. MacKay. 'He won't have liked that *at all*'.

She laughed.

'It's not that funny', said Janice, 'he is Malcolm's brother after all. And up until now, I thought I'd been getting on with all the family'.

'Oh, don't fret lass', said the older lady, 'deep down his own parents know what he's like. And the important thing is', she added, 'he is not like his brother'.

As she drove back towards Inverarish, she was glad she didn't have to drive past him again. People were right though. He was good looking and she could see what the physical attraction was. There also was something appealing in how sure of himself he was.
A little caught up in her thoughts, she almost failed to spot the tractor coming round the bend, but the driver had stopped to enable her to get into the passing place safely. She realised it was Malcolm.

Winding down the window again, she shouted towards his cab.

'THANK GOODNESS IT'S YOU!'

He had turned the engine off so that he could hear her, but she shouted so loudly he was pretty sure half of Raasay must have heard her.

She laughed and tried again.

'I was saying', she giggled, 'I'm glad it's you'.

'And I'm glad it's you too', he smiled in response.

'I just met your brother earlier', she informed him.

'Oh', said Malcolm, a bit hesitantly.

'He seemed to think I was checking up on him', she advised.

'Oh, I hope he wasn't bumptious to you', he said, but deep down he hoped a little that he had been, as he didn't want her falling for him.

'Och no, it doesn't really matter', she said. 'I think for a while Malcolm, we are going to find it hard to meet up' she said, 'with all the social distancing requirements we've to stick to'.

He knew it, she had fallen for his older brother's looks and was now looking at ways of cooling off their relationship.

'We could meet like this?' he suggested.

'Yes, we could', she laughed.

'You are usually passing here at quarter past eleven each day', he informed.

'Malcolm MacLean!' she exclaimed, 'have you been watching my every step?'

She laughed.

'Okay. Eleven fifteen tomorrow it is'.

She blew him a kiss and drove off, and then felt a little silly having done so.

'Take this down to your brother for me', his mother said to Malcolm, handing him a plastic box with lunch items in it once he returned home.

'And when you're at it, tell him dinner will be at five when you see him please', his father shouted after him.

As he left by the small entrance door, Christina turned to her husband.

'It's so nice to have everyone back together again and getting on so well. It's just like when they were younger', she said.

Coming down from the roadside he walked through the potato field, carrying the small plastic boxes. He noticed how the potatoes were showing and with the weather turning a bit milder, and with the root development, he thought it was maybe time to remove the enviro-fleece from them. Then again, he thought more wisely of it, thinking of how the frost can come quite suddenly overnight.

He remembered the night in the late autumn when he had been ploughing the field, and he caught something in the plough. By the time he had fumbled his way in the darkness to fix and release it from a deeply embedded stone, he jumped back in and thought that the tractor cab window had steamed up. It turned out that in the half hour he had been out of the cab, and despite any heat it may have generated, the cab window had in fact partly frozen over.

Reaching the glamping pod, he rapped on the window. His brother came out and took the sandwich boxes from him, sitting on one of the two benches that were located on each side of the entrance.

'Not exactly warm out here', he said to his younger sibling.

'No, but it's mild enough for the potatoes to grow some more', Malcolm observed. 'Oh, and Dad asked me to remind you dinner is at five'.

'As if I'd forget', scoffed Alex. 'It's never changed, except on a bloody Sunday'.

'I'm surprised…', Malcolm began, but stopped.

'Go on, what were you going to say', encouraged Alex.

'I was just going to say I'm surprised you came back after all you said about the island before you left last time', said Malcolm.

'I've nowhere else to go mate. There's a pandemic doing the rounds in case you haven't noticed'.

'You know both Mum and Dad called you quite a few times over the last couple of months, and they never heard a word from you', Malcolm protested.

'My phone, it had a problem', Alex replied dryly. 'And what's it to you?' he added. 'I never got a call from you once if you were so concerned'.

'How do you know if your phone was broken?' Malcolm shot back.

A short period of silence fell between them.

'And I bumped into Fiona last Friday', he added.

'Oh, that'd be nice for you. Were you swooning?' said Alex sarcastically.

'I don't swoon Alex. I've got my own girlfriend to think about thank you', replied Malcolm.

'I heard', said Alex, 'in fact I think I bumped into her this morning'.

'Yes, I heard that', said Malcolm.

'Oh, so it was her? The nurse'.

'Yes, she's one of the community nurses', Malcolm confirmed.

'I'd maybe watch her', Alex suggested.

'What do you mean?' asked Malcom suspiciously.

'Well, she's got a bit of a mouth on her. A bit of a bossy bitch you've got yourself there'.

Malcolm rose to his feet feeling indignant.

'Sod off Alex. You don't know what you're talking about'.

'Ah, have you not laid her then? Is that what it is?' said Alex smuttily.

Malcolm stepped towards him pushing his elder brother on the shoulder.

'Who's the big man now?' mocked his elder brother, rising to his feet and pushing his brother backwards causing him to stumble off the front of the glamping pod.

His younger brother pulled himself up to his full height, but by then Alex had hit him solidly on the cheek bone, causing his younger sibling to stumble.

'I can't believe you did that Alex', he shouted.

Alex felt some remorse as he had never really struck his brother before, except for pretend fights when they were younger. He had actually drawn blood.

Malcolm turned to walk away, and Alex sprung down from the pod and grabbed his brother by his shoulder. They turned around to face one another.

'What, you going to try again Alex?' Malcolm asked, his head leaning in towards his brother, 'cause if you do, you might just it back this time, twice as hard'.

Alex was more cautious, as he thought his younger brother was built a lot more solidly than he was.

'Look, I didn't mean it', said Alex. 'I came back to get away from all the drink and drugs in Glasgow, it turns you a bit mental, you see'.

'That's not an excuse Alex. It's not an excuse for the way you treat Mum and Dad. It's not an excuse for the way you treat Fiona, and you're not going to speak about Janice that way either'.

'I know' said Alex trying to placate his brother, who was angrier than he had probably ever seen him before.
'Sometimes things get a grip of you and you don't always know what you're doing'.

Malcolm turned and walked away, but turned back again to reply.

'You know Alex, I've looked up to you all these years, but God knows only why. We are all responsible for the choices we make, nothing forces us to do what we don't want to do'.

And with that turn of eloquent speech, which in Malcolm's case was very rare indeed, he turned around and walked off through the field.

Alex was glad he had calmed him down. He thought he was going to hit him back at one point. He stood there looking on as his brother reached the roadside.

When Malcolm returned home his mother looked at him aghast in horror.

'You're bleeding', she exclaimed loudly which was enough to rouse his father's attention.

'What happened son?' he asked.

'Oh, just Alex, surely that doesn't come as a surprise?'

'Well, it does actually', his father protested. 'What happened. Were you fighting?'

'If you mean did he hit me, then yes that's obviously what happened', retorted Malcolm.

'And why ever did he hit you?' his mother asked in a dramatic voice.

'It doesn't matter Mum, it really doesn't', he said pulling himself away from her as she approached him with a cloth to dab below his eye.

'You might need a stitch for that', his father said. 'Now what were the pair of you fighting about?'

'I'm not going to get a stitch', said Malcom looking alarmed. 'What does it matter what we were arguing about?

'Well, it does matter. You can't be taking pot shots at each other for no reason now, can you?'

'I never took a pot shot!' Malcolm protested. 'You're always quick to defend Alex. He tells you how bad the island is, so you give him one of the glamping pods. He bad mouths you and Mum, and you welcome him back with open arms. You serve him everything up on a dish and he takes it, and more. He bats his eyelids at a woman and they all swoon over him'.

'Ah, a bit jealous are we?' his father suggested. Malcolm glared at him and going through to the small passageway that led to his room, slammed the door behind him.

'I've never seen him like this', his mother remarked, sounding worried.

'Oh, give him ten minutes and it'll blow over,' said her husband. 'He can blow quite hot. The other week he was using a winch on the tractor and it got stuck, and he flew into a rage until he managed to release it. Ten minutes later and he was his normal calm self again'.

'Oh', said his wife, not so sure that he would be.

But true enough, ten minutes later he reappeared and calmly informed them he was going to call in at the surgery in case his cheek needed a stitch.

When Malcolm reached the surgery, he read the note in the window. It was only open on a Wednesday from nine in the morning to twelve mid-day, so he had to call an out-of-hours number.

As he approached the nurses' house, as he'd been directed to, he was embarrassed to find it was Janice who was the on-call nurse and who answered the door.

Although he was her boyfriend, she tried to remain wholly professional in her approach, but could only maintain the façade for a while.

'What was it that struck you?' she asked.

He did not want to tell her, but she was quick on his trail.

'Was it your brother?'

'Yes', he said giving a one word reply.

'But why Malcolm?' she pressed on, and before long he was recounting the whole story to him.

'Well Malcolm MacLean' she said at one point sounding a little indignant, 'you don't need to be defending my good name to anyone'.

She thought there was something quite touching in the fact that he had, and having heard what Malcolm had said about the way his brother treated his girlfriend and talked about his parents, she was surprised to find that she kind of wished in a strange sort of way that he had decked him. In fact, she knew his girlfriend lived close by.

'You did the right thing though', she consoled him, 'walking away, that is. Now you'll be pleased to hear all we need to do is put a steri-strip on this. The needle can wait for another day!'

They laughed.

LAMENTATIONS

It was just like any of the other days that she had had on the island. It started off with the two nurses on duty dividing up the patients, and once again, Janice found she would be seeing everyone north of the big house. The only real difference was that as she got to know the road better, she knew she didn't quite have to rush as much, as she used to in her first few months on the island.

She saw Mrs. MacKay, and wondered what she was going to do, as her visits there always took her past Malcolm, who was waiting patiently at the layby to say hello to her. He was always there, even if she was running late, which she thought was very sweet of him. But now Mrs. MacKay's leg was almost healed, she doubted whether or not she'd be even calling on her again much after next week.

The wound below Malcolm's eye had also closed up quite nicely and in a few weeks she was sure it would be barely noticeable. She wondered why his brother was so mean towards him, and felt like giving him a piece of her mind if she ever passed him on the road again.

Mealtimes for the next few evenings following the argument had been a tense affair at the MacLean household. Little was discussed by the two brothers, and nothing was said between them both. But Mrs. MacLean, forever the mediator, always managed to do just that and serve as a go between to create a semblance of fraternity where there was in fact none.

Malcolm had also avoided tending the potatoes, or even checking on them, as he had no wish to go to the potato field and find himself in his brother's hostile company again.

He used to feel sorry for him, having to go to the mainland to study and train, with a view to eventually working his way back to the island. That must be hard, he had thought, and there was the stress of his exams too. But the sympathy he had had dissolved, and he no longer felt much warmth for him, particularly following their sharp exchange of words the other day.

'So how are you getting your shopping Mrs. MacKay?' asked Janice.

'It's not easy, but the store is very good. They will drop some things by for you my dear', she informed the young nurse.

As she drove home she stopped at the layby to see her other patient.

'Come on Rocky, look up. Don't be shy', she said jokingly to Malcolm. 'Yes, that has closed up quite nicely. You're lucky, cause if it had been any deeper, it would have been a needle and thread job'.

Malcolm looked away towards the sea.

'Look', he said pointing.

'What is it, what do you see?' she asked, unsure of what he had discovered as she could not see anything.

'Look it's getting closer', he said.

'It's well seen your boxing hasn't affected your eyesight', she laughed. 'I can't see anything', though as she said it, she could indeed see a black speck on the water.

'That's the lifeboat', he informed her.

'Okay, I'll take your word for it, but it just looks like a black dot to me'.

A few minutes passed and the orange facing of the craft became obvious.

'Looks like they are heading this way', he informed. 'Maybe you'll be needed Janice'.

'Yes, you are right', she said. 'I better go back down to Inverarish just in case'.

Winding up her window she blew him a kiss through the glass and sped off. As she entered the nurses' cottage she was met by her colleague Margaret.

'I'm just going back up the road to wait for the fire engine', she said.

'The fire engine?' asked Janice.

'Yes, they are coming to take a patient to the lifeboat to transfer her to the A&E at Portree, and then they can decide what to do'.

'How what's happened?' she asked.

'The young girl, she had an asthma attack', her colleague informed her. 'We needed to get oxygen from the health centre for her, but she's not right. It's not alleviating her laboured breathing'.

'Can I do anything?' asked Janice.

'Eh …yes. Come up with me. It's not the best of times I know, but it never is. You can meet the lifeboat crew and the paramedics, as unfortunately they will become a familiar sight to you, as this is the way we have to transport people to the hospital quickly when the ferry won't do'.

Janice and Margaret walked up past the community run shop and post office, and went around the corner. They knocked on the door of the little terraced house and the door opened. Without a word, an older woman ushered them inside, and led them up the stairs.

As they entered the young woman's bedroom, Janice noticed she was managing to hold the face mask independently to extract the oxygen, which was a good sign, but she could hear the wheeziness every time she inhaled and exhaled. A few moments later they were joined by the fire crew who carried the young woman down the stairs and into the small fire and rescue vehicle. Margaret and Janice jumped in alongside her.

'Don't worry, we haven't got far to go', said her elder colleague to reassure her patient.

As they approached the harbour they were met by the Lifeboat and two paramedics from Portree, who carefully took the young woman onto the craft, and placed the patient between themselves. In a matter of a few minutes they were off, and the orange craft soon turned into a black dot once again.

'Do you want a lift back up the road?' asked the fireman.

'No, I think we'll just walk back', said Margaret, looking for the opportunity to unwind a little.

'That's a shame', said Janice. 'I hope she's okay'.

'Yes, I hope so', said Margaret, and the pair of them walked up past the big house and along the road past the distillery.
'Normally you'd get a small crowd for this sort of thing', said Margaret, 'but today, with the distillery being closed and with the lockdown, there are few if any people about. Mind you', she added managing a laugh, 'the whole island will soon know what's been going on'.

They took the low road down towards the park, past the school, medical centre and the new community centre.

'There was meant to be a ceilidh on this weekend, but as you can imagine everything is up in the air just now', said Margaret.

Indeed, it was not just the ceilidh that was up in the air, for once the patient reached Portree and was transferred with the paramedics onto the ambulance, on arrival at the Hospital the decision was made to transfer her further by helicopter, to Raigmore Hospital in Inverness.

Malcolm who still did not relish the engagement, came through for the dinner at five o'clock. He was feeling a little better about it though.

'Look', said his father to him earlier in the day, 'it's just the way your brother is'.

'As I said the other night Dad. He's first to tell you how everything about the croft sucks; how island life sucks the lifeblood from his veins – his words, not mine- and how he doesn't want the life of domesticity that Mum or you have. It's almost as if no matter what you do, it's never good enough for him. And he gets everything'.

'That's it boy, do speak your mind', smirked his father. 'But that's not all lad, is it?'

'I don't know what you mean', Malcolm responded looking uncertain.

'You missed the bit about the women'.

'What bit?' his son retorted.

'The bit about women swooning after him. That's what you said, wasn't it?' his father asserted.

'Yes, well I suppose right enough. It's true. He treats Fiona like shit and he just looks down on them, yet they all come running', protested Malcolm.

'I sense a little bit of insecurity underneath all you're saying lad', his father suggested.
'I don't think Janice is the type that would fall for him, if that is what you are worried about'.

'I'm sure not!' exclaimed Malcolm in anger at the fact that she had been introduced to the conversation at all.

'I hit a nerve there I see', said his father. 'Well let me put it like this son. If your Janice, or let's say any other woman you were dating were to fall for your brother, it wouldn't really say that much about her then, now would it?'

'I…I suppose not', thought Malcolm aloud.

'Well stop letting the fear of it eat away at you. And as for your brother getting everything, it's not true either. You don't know it, but I might as well tell you, if only to make you see that it's not true. I assigned the croft over to you, so that when I die, the tenancy will pass on to you'.

'Oh…but I never wanted, nor expected that Dad', said Malcolm subdued.

'I know you didn't. But it is yours because I know your heart is in the right place and that you will look after it. But don't be too down on your brother, though he should never have struck you. Maybe he has to find out for himself what's important in life, and maybe son he's just on a different part of the road than you are'.

The evening meal passed peaceably. Malcolm seemed more relaxed and although he did not speak to his brother, he did manage to feign interest in the response to his father's question to Alex of how his brother's studies were progressing. That was before the meal was rudely interrupted by the landline phone and which his mother answered.

'Now I've got the dongle and can access the internet from the pod', Alex informed, 'I am able to access the documents I need to complete the assignment I have been working on'.

'I see', said his mother to the person to whom she was on the phone. 'Yes, yes, I think I'll do that. Thanks for letting me know'.

'Well, I'm going to remove the plates boys, given your mother has done all the hard work of preparing this for us', their father informed them.

'I'll give you a hand', said Malcolm volunteering his services which his father was grateful for.

'Come outside for some air dear', said Christina MacLean to her elder son, Alex.

'I've just come from the air outside', Alex half-heartedly protested.

'No come', his mother insisted, which sounded more like an instruction rather than a request, which was most unlike her. He expected she was going to try to scold him verbally about the fight he had had with Malcolm the other day.

'I need to tell you something', she said to him once they had exited the small croft house door.

Here we go, he thought.

'Fiona, she's dead son', she said putting her hand on his shoulder.

'What?' exclaimed Alex taken aback at the unexpected nature of the news she just told him.

'Fiona is dead Alex. She died when they were transferring her to the hospital in Inverness. They think it was due to her asthma, though they can't say if this new virus had anything to do with it or not'.

'Dead?' said Alex repeating it. 'Dead?'

'Yes dear, Fiona is dead', she motioned to hug him, but he stretched out his arm to keep her distant.

'Well, I never expected that one', said Alex and he started to walk up the path in deep thought.

His mother decided to let him go. She thought that maybe he needed the space to grieve in his own way, which was very perceptive, as that is exactly what he needed to do.

He headed off towards the road and walked down it a little and towards the potato field, but rather than turning off to go to his glamping pod, he continued on the road down towards the big house in the direction of Inverarish.

As these things do in small island communities, the news of the death of one of the small island's population spread across the north, south and breadth of the island in no time at all. The fact that Fiona was so young too, gave it an added poignancy.
So, it came as no surprise that when he reached Duncan's house at the Old Post Office, that he had already heard the news. He found him in the back garden working on a garden shed.

'I'm sorry mate. I really am', Duncan consoled putting down his tools. 'Here, have a whisky', he offered and passed a bottle that sat on a counter top he was building as part of the interior to the shed. He gave it to his friend who gulped some straight down without much thought, or caution for that matter.

'Here, go easy mate', his friend cautioned.

'Sorry', said Alex in a subdued manner looking at the contents of the bottle.

'Go on, have some more', said Duncan mindful of his friend's need, but also discreetly looking anxiously out of the corner of his eye at the contents of the bottle.

As the evening wore on he had reason to look more anxious, as the bottle was soon drained of its contents. They were both a bit the worse for wear, and their speech was not always coherent.

'Aye, she was a fine lass', Duncan consoled.

'Prettiest school' said Alex before correcting himself, 'prettiest *in* the school'.

'Starlight night', remarked Duncan looking skywards, not too sure what else to say by way of consolation.

'There's no stars you daft basket', exclaimed Alex, 'it's raining'.

'You maybe don't see stars Alex…but I do', his friend protested. 'What is it they say?'

There was a period of silence.

'Well, what do they say?' asked Alex, bemused at the lack of elucidation from his friend.

'I don't know', said Duncan.

'Well...', exclaimed Alex, but was interrupted.

'Shut up, shut up. I know, I know. One looked and saw stars...the other looked and saw mud'.

'That doesn't even make sense, you daft big basket', Alex remarked going to push his friend on his shoulder, but instead slightly overbalancing and missed him. Fortunately, his arm landed on a large empty water butt that was sitting upright in the middle of the lawn, that was waiting to be installed.

'I know, I know', said Duncan, 'shut up a moment'.

'I never said anything', laughed Alex.

'Wait a minute, wait a minute. I've got it...', but another period of silence.

'Well...', said Alex impatiently.

'Shut up will you...one looked down...and saw stars. No there were two men', Duncan suggested tentatively.

'Where?' asked Alex.

'No, no goddamn it. Shut up, shut up!' his friend exclaimed, before adding, 'There were two men. One looked down and saw mud, the other looked up and saw stars'.

'Where was that?' asked Alex.

'Damned if I know', said Duncan laughing at his own ineptitude. Then he sounded alarmed. 'I've no more whisky you know?'

'That's not like you', joked Alex.

'I know, I know', said Duncan, 'but it's serious. The shop is out of stock because they announced the bars are closing, and Raasay House is now closed too – so there's none. There's no alcohol and there's no pub'.

The shock of what he was saying seemed to have a sobering effect upon him.

'That's why I'm building this pub here', he proclaimed.

'And how's that going to solve the problem? asked Alex.

'Well, I've never been to a pub that's empty before', said Duncan.

'But if there's no alcohol Duncan…', Alex started to reason before changing tack for loss of concentration.
'I can't mind what I was going to say now, but yes, they'll need alcohol for the funeral', Alex exclaimed emphatically, to which his friend readily consented.

'But what the hell are we to do in the meantime?' protested Duncan.

'An island with its own bloody distillery', quipped Alex, 'and you can't get alcohol'.

'Let's go inside', Duncan invited, 'I think I have some lager in the cupboard'.

As they walked back indoors, Alex's head caught the small entrance to the Old Post Office and he landed on the ground. As his friend turned around, he noticed that he was laid out cold on the ground, so he dragged him into the sitting room, and left him lying there on the floor in front of the fire where he knew he would keep warm.

POTATO HEAD

It was still early and the sun was rising when Malcolm took a walk down to the Potato field. He hoped he would not disturb his brother, as he really had no wish to make conversation with him.

The soil was quite wet from the rain the previous night, and he was sure there had been some marked growth in the last few days. The rain would undoubtedly have helped them on greatly, he thought. So, he spent the first hour of his morning rolling up the enviro-fleece he had used to cover the tubers. He looked at his watch and seeing it was around eight in the morning, he decided to head for home for breakfast.

There was still no light on in the glamping pod. In fact, the small blinds his Mum had installed in it to give his brother privacy, not that there would be anyone looking in asides from probably himself when attending to the potatoes, were still open.
That's odd, thought Malcolm, but he had no desire to pursue the matter further and started to walk up the field to reach the roadside.

A mile and a half away further up that road, his brother began to awaken slowly.
He rubbed his head as it was sore, and he noticed he had blood on his hand.

'Eh Duncan', he said, but his friend was long gone, having been up early to make it in time to complete the checks before launching the first ferry.

Alex walked through to the bathroom which was not the cleanest environment.

As he strained to look at himself in the mirror due to his headache, he noticed he had a graze across his forehead. He muttered something about stupidity, before returning to the sitting room where he found an empty whisky bottle and several empty cans of lager. He remembered the whisky, the rain, but he didn't recall drinking any lager. It wasn't really his thing. He rubbed his head again and it felt like a misshapen potato.

'I do hope he was alright last night', his mother was saying to his father over the breakfast table at the croft house in Oscaig.

'He'll be fine', his father insisted, 'but it will have come as a shock. If I know him, he will probably have been drowning his sorrows. He'll probably not even give Fiona, poor girl, much thought after the funeral is over'.

His mother noted the unusually acerbic tone in her husband's voice, but was not too sure about his conclusion.

When Malcolm came in, she asked him if he had seen his brother this morning.

'No', he responded, and no-one chose to pursue the matter any further with him as he sat down to breakfast.

The surgery was quiet and there was only a half hour left of opening. Janice, as one of the nurses on duty on the island, would spend the Wednesday morning in the surgery from nine o'clock to mid-day, picking up any urgent referrals from the G.P.
They had to restrict their appointments to urgent cases only due to the restrictions caused by the coronavirus.

Donning her face mask, she was a little taken aback when at half past eleven she was asked to see her first patient of the day, only to find it was someone she recognized.

'Morning', she said inviting him in.

'It's my head', he said, 'I think I have split it'.

'And how did you do that?' she asked, worried that he might have had another go at Malcolm.

'I think I tripped and fell', he said.

'You think?' she asked a little surprised he was so unsure about what had happened.

'Yes, I was drinking, and I think I fell over and cut it', he informed her feeling a little resentful that she should question him.

'Well let me take a look', she said motioning his head back gently.

He felt her soothing touch. His brother had done well for himself he thought, punching well above his weight. As she turned round to pick up some utensils, he ran his eyes up and down her legs.

'I'm going to bathe your forehead in a little saline solution, and then I'll see what we need to do next', she informed, as she dabbed his head with some wet cotton wool.

For a moment she thought he was vulnerable and she could take advantage of the situation by being a little rougher than she would normally be with her patients, but she knew she was a professional who was there to treat everyone to the best of her abilities who were in need. He felt he was warming to her touch as she examined his forehead further and stroked his hair away from it gently.

'Well?' he asked abruptly.

'I'm going to have to put some steri-strips on it. It'll be painless', she reassured him.

She was about to add that he and his brother were depleting her roll of steri-strip more than any other household on the island, but she thought better of it.

'I hope you look after my little brother', he quipped. 'He's not that experienced you know', he added sarcastically.

'Oh, I thought he was *very* experienced the other night', she shot back, knowing only too well they had done no more than ever exchange kisses and hold hands.

'Mmmm…', mumbled Alex, 'I presume that is what you mean when you ask people about taking their daily exercise!' he implied smuttily.

'You must be very sad to lose Fiona', Janice suggested.
'There now', she added with some relief in her voice when applying the final strip, 'that's you all done'.

He rose from the chair without even a thanks in his voice and left the surgery.

Janice heaved a heavy sigh of relief.

As he walked down towards the big house and towards the pier, he noticed that the ferry was just getting in. He thought about how he and Fiona would in their final few years at the High School in Portree, tread this very same path to the ferry day in and day out. Sometimes she wanted to hold hands, but he wasn't really into that and for a moment he wondered why.

As he walked towards the end of the pier and the ramp of the roll-on roll-off ferry lowered, he could hear and then see that his friend was having an altercation with two passengers on the ferry. He walked further down the pier and onto the end of the ramp and overheard his friend telling the two men,

'you should never have got on board in the first place'.

'What's it to you?' said the taller of the two men aggressively pointing at Duncan.

'This is a lifeline service only!' exclaimed Duncan.

'Yes, it's my life – not yours', the other man responded rather stupidly.

By now the captain of the ferry was on deck and was joining in, but he remained calm and polite in his explanation.

'You don't understand', he told the two men, 'if the virus gets on to the island the whole population could very easily catch it within a matter of days. We don't have the resources to deal with it'.

Now this heated exchange began to look as if it could turn into fisticuffs, so Alex walked up the ramp and made his height and presence known.

'You heard them', he said, 'lifeline only. That means if you *value* your life, you'll take the next ferry back'.

Realising they were outnumbered, the two men walked off in disgust.

'You'll need tourists to survive', one shouted back as they walked up the pier.

'Thanks for that', said Duncan, 'I thought for a wee moment there that things were going to turn nasty. Jeez, look at your head man'.

'I know, I went up to the surgery and got patched up. Did I fall or something?'

'You stuck the head in the door frame if that is what you mean', his friend laughed.

The captain approached them.

'Thanks for that Alex. Sorry to hear about your woman', he said.

'Aye, thanks', said Alex.

'Come up to the house', Duncan suggested.

'What, are you not going back?' asked Alex confused, as the water seemed quite calm.

'No, we are not due back on board till after five tonight. We are on a restricted timetable'.

When they reached the house Duncan offered his friend some chips and to fry up some sausages.

'I think it would turn my stomach at this time in the morning', said Alex.

'It's now afternoon' said his friend.

'I don't know how you can eat all that fried food, particularly after last night', Alex insisted.

FEELINGS OF LOSS

Malcolm disliked Wednesdays as he knew this was the day he would not see Janice, particularly at the moment with all the social distancing requirements, but especially on a Wednesday as she was on surgery duty in the morning once a week.

He had collected all the enviro-fleece he had removed earlier that morning from the potatoes, which he had dragged to the roadside for collecting later. He knew he still had the pleasure of the hen houses to clean.
Might as well do all the grubby chores today, he thought to himself dejectedly.

His mother had been telling them at the lunch table that she had taken Alex down some sandwiches but that he wasn't in the glamping pod when she called, so she left them on one of the seats at its entrance. She was concerned he was okay, particularly following the death of Fiona. She also told them how it had been decided that only family could attend the funeral, because of the new social distancing requirements and she wondered how Alex would feel about that when he heard the news.

Mrs. MacLean also told them how she had two men at the door, which would have surprised her at the best of times, but 'at this time', she had exclaimed.
They had asked her about taking two of the glamping pods for a few nights, but she had given them short shrift and told them that they could not think of taking anyone in until the pandemic was over.

'Ah, it shows you there is a market for them though', said her husband in a self-satisfied manner.

'You're awfully quiet today Malcolm', said his mother.

'No, just thinking of the hen houses', he responded and rose from the dinner table with a view to cleaning them out.

'A nasty job', said his mother to her husband when her son had left the house.

'I think it's Wednesday that's the problem Christina', the man of the house surmised.

'Wednesday?' asked his wife.

'Aye, Wednesday', he said. 'There'll be no *smooching* on a Wednesday', he laughed as did his wife in response.

Back at the Old Post Office concerns of a different kind were being expressed.

'I have no idea how we can get any booze', sighed Duncan. 'The shop has not got any, and they say what comes in next week will be given over for Fiona's funeral. Though that will not be much', he added.

'How so?' asked Alex.

'Well, you can only have close family there', said his friend.

'Why?' asked Alex not thinking it through.

'Because of the social distancing regulations. In theory, you and I shouldn't even be in the same house, not that I mind, and you're only meant to go out in twos.

'Well, we'll have just to have our own wake or something to remember her by', said Alex, a little taken aback having not thought about the implications of the pandemic.

'And that's why we need booze Alex. There is none!' protested his friend.

There was a long period of silence.

'Oh, bollocks!' Alex exclaimed.

'T'is not bollocks Alex', insisted Duncan, 'not if you think it through'.

'It's you that's not thinking it through Duncan', said Alex and without breath added, 'you've got a whole bloody distillery on the island'.

'Aye, but it's closed remember Alex. And anyway, all that they have is called "While We Wait", so it's not ready yet'.

'Don't be such a plonker Duncan. The whisky is called "While you Wait"', said Alex.

'"While *We* Wait"', corrected his friend.

'"While We Wait", or whatever you want to call it', said Alex, 'it doesn't mean you *have to* wait. We don't want "While We Wait"'.

'What you talking about man?' his friend exclaimed. 'It's a damn good dram, and why would they call it "While We Wait" if you didn't have to wait?'

'Oh, fuck me' said Alex in exasperation. 'Listen. Just because the whisky is called "While you Wait"… "While We Wait"', he added correcting himself, 'It's not an instruction!'

'What do you mean?' asked Duncan, whose brain was feeling pickled.

'The whisky is released at the end of the year, which means there are barrels of the stuff sitting in the warehouse at the distillery', suggested Alex.

'Oh, I don't know', informed Duncan, 'they opened a new warehouse in the village last year and that's why they have "While We Wait"'.

'Look, will you just forget "While We Wait" just for a moment. Put it out of your head' said Alex completely exasperated. He took a deep breath. 'Look I know, but have you been on-line?' said Alex. 'They have a few barrels there in the distillery maturing for the visitors to see and sample'.

'I don't go on-line, but yes …you have a point. They're not waiting'.

'Exactly. All we need to do is to go in there and get one', Alex stated.

'And how do we do that?' asked Duncan innocently.

'We have to steal it, Duncan. Break in and take it', Alex suggested.

'Oh, but there is Ian, the watchman, Alex. He'll know it's missing'.

'Aye', said Alex, 'but not if you replace it'.

'Replace it?' asked Duncan looking confused.

'Aye, listen. If we break in, steal the whisky, remove the contents and then put the barrel back, then no-one will know it has been stolen'.

'They will if it's bloody empty Alex'.

'Ever heard of the angels' share?' asked Alex.

'It'll be a bloody big angel that drinks all that', his friend protested.

'Look, if we put it back, remove the contents, then it'll just look like any old barrel. There's no tourists there to sample it, and it will be weeks before anyone tries to drink from it. So how can anyone think we stole it?'

'And how do we remove the contents, Alex?' asked Duncan. 'I can't drink a whole 250 litre barrel in a night, not even with your help. And I doubt for that matter we'd be in a fit state to put it back after drinking all that'.

'Don't be daft. We'd empty and store it, and return the empty barrel', Alex informed.

'And where the hell are we going to store 250 litres of malt whisky Alex?' his friend asked.

Alex stood up.

'Come with me', he said and they walked out the back door of the Old Post Office and into the garden. On this occasion Alex remembered to duck. When they returned to the house they firmed up on their plan.

'Meet me at the pier when the boat comes in', said Duncan.

'What time?' asked Alex.

'There only is one ferry this evening, so we'll be back and finished just after six thirty', Duncan stated.

'And do you honestly think the Captain will be up for it?' asked Alex.

'Aye', said Duncan, 'he is feeling the loss just as acutely as you or I'.

THE BIRDS

Alex was careful to ensure he was home for dinner at five o'clock. His mother expressed concern about his head but readily accepted his excuse that he had tripped on the road and scraped it on the tarmac, after he had left her last night.

'I had to go to the surgery and get it taped up', he told the gathering at the dinner table. 'In fact, I saw your woman', he said pointedly to his brother.

Malcolm merely lifted his head in a bare acknowledgement, while feeling slightly resentful that Alex would have had the chance to see her today, while he had not.

When the large wooden Napoleon clock on the mantlepiece chimed seven, an hour more than what the actual time was, Alex excused himself after unusually helping to clear and dry the dishes. He used to decline this task on principle, on the basis that his parents should own a dishwasher and not have to resort to such antiquated habits.

As he walked down towards the big house, he rehearsed in his mind the plan he had hit upon. He could see no reason why it should not work. Everyone on the island knew that Ian, the watchman, started his night watch at ten through to eight in the morning. But they also knew in Ian's case, that the term 'night watch' was a misnomer, for everyone knew that he enjoyed his food.

'Aye, I need to go and grab some dinner', said the Captain. 'Noodles and nutloaf'.

'I'm going up the road too', informed Duncan. He offered Alex dinner. 'I'll make some chips and fry up some sausages'.

'That's what you had for lunch', said Alex shaking his head. 'Not a vegetable to be seen between your plate and Portree!'
Both he and the Captain laughed.

They all agreed to go their separate ways until later. Alex would call in first at the old Post Office where Duncan lived, at nine twenty. The Captain would then follow on at nine thirty exactly.

It was late evening when Janice finally sat down for dinner. It had been a long day. It had started off quietly at the surgery with just one patient to be seen, Malcolm's brother, but in the afternoon she had attended the patients in Inverarish. When she finished at five o'clock, she was about to make dinner when she had been visited by three women, all of whom had lots of queries about what were the symptoms of coronavirus, and how they should best protect everyone in their houses from it.

She had remained polite, but did strongly urge them not to go out together as a threesome but to remain within their own households. Despite the death of the young girl, Fiona, which was confirmed as being due to asthma and not coronavirus related, there appeared to be no-one on the island that they knew of, exhibiting the kind of symptoms that were consistent with having the virus.
This seemed to reassure the anxious mothers.

Janice enjoyed island life, but the nurses' cottage was right in the middle of the terraced houses, and the nurses were accessible to everyone night and day, whether they were on duty or not. Fortunately, there was the rota where two of them were on duty, while two were off, but it made little difference as people did not draw these distinctions.

It was now near seven o'clock when she sat down. Any thought that still lingered of going out for a walk for exercise after dinner was soon dispelled, when she looked out of the kitchen window. The wind was picking up and it had started to rain heavily.

Malcolm sat in his room flicking through some new books that the Heritage Trust had produced. He liked to know about his heritage and the island's history. His family had been cleared from the iconic clearance village called, 'Hallaig', which the famous Gaelic poet Sorley MacLean had written about. Sharing the same surname, it came as little surprise to him to learn, when he was younger, that they were in fact blood line relatives, though he never had the chance to meet him.

But he couldn't quite settle himself and concentrate for long enough on the book of place names. He kept thinking of how Alex had seen Janice when he was not able to do so. He thought of them together, and the thought of it went deep down and into the pit of his stomach, that it made him feel sick.

He began to work himself into a frenzy, and he had a flash in his mind of his brother lying beside her, and he tried to drive it hard from his mind. But as hard as he tried, it kept resurfacing, the image becoming stronger the more he tried to resist it.

Finally, he jumped off his bed and grabbed his jacket.

'I'm off to check the potatoes', he announced and walked up to the roadside and along the road. As he turned down into the potato field, he noticed that his brother's light was not on, and the sun was not far from setting.

He so wanted to tell him how everything he touched made it unsavoury, and how ever since he came back to the island how he had adversely affected his own life, Fiona's life, and he wasn't going to let him interfere in Janice's life either. And then he remembered what she had said about walking away, and what his Dad had said to him about 'the fear of it' eating away at him. He turned around having reached within ten metres of the glamping pod and having thought better of it, returned to the croft house.

'Your Janice called when you were out', his mother was quick to tell him.

'Did she say anything?' he asked.

'Yes', his mother replied, teasing him by not deliberately elaborating any further.

'Come on Mum for goodness' sake, what did she say then?' he asked impatiently.

'No need to get hot under the collar about it, Malcolm', she said a little taken aback at his hostile reaction. 'She just asked how we were all doing, how you were today, and if you'd give her a call back'.

He was already doing so before she finished her answer.

His father did his best not to eavesdrop, but it is hard when you are reading and someone is talking. Later he confided quietly to his wife.

'And I heard him say to her, what are you eating. Bloody hell Christina, in my day I'd be asking you what you were wearing'.

They both laughed.

Alex looked at his mobile phone, and as Director of Operations he made sure he was at Duncan's front door at precisely nine twenty. So, when he went in, he was surprised to see the Captain already there.

'I came early to share what was left in my bottle', he laughed holding it up.

'There's nothing in it', said Alex looking puzzled.

'Not now', laughed the Captain, 'but there was earlier'.

'And there soon will be later' added Duncan joining in the merriment.

'Guys', said Alex, 'we need to be stone cold sober to pull this off. It's like working with a delicate piece of machinery. You can't do it while drunk'.

'What, like drive a boat?' laughed the Captain, and he and Duncan shared a hearty laugh.

'Okay, okay', said Alex feeling a little perturbed. He followed Duncan into the kitchen, the wash hand basin now overflowing with dishes and whisky glasses.

'Do you think he's fit enough to pull this off?' he asked his friend.

'Fit as a fiddle my man', said Duncan slapping him on the shoulder, clearly having shared in some of the same spirit.

'No, I mean is he altogether in terms of sobriety?' Alex asked.

'Yes, yes', said his friend, 'I've seen him much worse before'.

Hardly feeling consoled, Alex followed Duncan back into the sitting room.

'Right', he said. 'Show me how to use one of the walkie talkies'.

After some brief guidance from the Captain, which Alex was pleased to find was coherent, he reminded everyone of the plan.
The Captain went to leave the house, but Alex stopped him in his tracks and looked at both of his partners in crime.

'Do not use your real names or designation from the ferry when you speak into these, just in case anyone picks up the signal?' he said.

'Unlikely anyone will pick it up' said the Captain, 'but good advice'.

'Oh, and try and disguise what you are saying, so no-one thinks we're raiding the distillery and so that we're the only ones who can understand the real meaning of what is being said, okay?' added Alex as an afterthought.

'So, what shall we call one another?' asked Duncan.

'I don't know, be creative', said Alex. 'I'll be calling you both first, so I'll make up some name for both of you. First, I'll call the Captain, then you Duncan'.

He looked harassed as he studied his watch. 'Right, we need to think about taking up our positions'.

It was exactly nine forty. The Captain proceeded first round the corner and took up position lying on the ground behind the large tree in the distillery car park.

Duncan had the easier job. He simply had to go to his back-bedroom window and look across at the black paneled building at the side of the distillery's visitor centre, though unlike the Captain, he could not see the front entrance as clearly.

Alex proceeded up the road past the distillery and took up position between the hedges that concealed the path up to the Free Presbyterian church, to give him a clear view of the road. It was now nine forty-five, and if Ian was true to form his 4x4 should appear on the road within the next ten to fifteen minutes. He had to travel from Fearns in the south of the island. It was a wet and stormy night.

Alex didn't have to wait long. He fumbled in the dark for the walkie talkie, which despite its waterproof cover was still quite slimy.

'Noodle nut loaf, come in'.

'*Nut loaf?*' came the Captain's response. 'Why nut loaf?' he asked.

'It's what you ate for dinner. Now wheesch', said Alex irritated before snapping, 'target is in sight'.

'Copy that', said the Captain.

Alex put the walkie talkie to his mouth.

'Come in… deep-fry. Do you have visual?'

There was no response. He repeated it urgently.

'Is that me you are talking to Alex?' big Duncan asked. 'Why deep fry?'

'Cause that's all you eat, you fat bastard!', Alex exclaimed in anger that his name had been used. 'Now *call me something else* and tell me if you see the target', he insisted.

'Aye, I do that…Potato head'.

'Potato head. Fuck me', said Alex aloud, but was interrupted by the crackling of the communication device.

'Noodle nut loaf here. I can confirm the eagle has landed'.

Alex appeared from the side of the church building, and after checking the road for other cars or people walking by, he began to cautiously walk back down towards the distillery.

'Deep fry here. The Eagle has left his nest'.

What does that mean? thought Alex. He must mean he has left his car, he reasoned.

Meanwhile the Captain was unsure of how to describe Ian's next move, as Duncan had taken the wind out his sail.

'Eh, Nut loaf here. The Eagle has mated'.

'What the fuck dude?' shouted Alex at the walkie talkie, 'Can you repeat to Potato head over?'

'Nut loaf here' and with great precision as he said each word, the Captain explained, 'The Eagle has mated… *and is off to find her little chicks*'.

'Deep Fry here. Don't see any chicks from here, over'.

Alex stood there dumbfounded. He had not a clue what he meant.

'Eh, Nut loaf here. She is off to find food for her little chicks'.

Alex understood.

'Potato head here. Copy that'.

The walkie talkie crackled again.

'Deep Fry here. How many chicks has she got, over?'

'Potato head here, there are no *fuckin'* chicks for God's sake. Meet at the rendezvous point and maintain radio silence, over'.

'Deep fry, copy that'.

'Nut loaf, copy that'.

Alex walked down towards the garage type building and stood with his back to the built-up wall with turf on it. The Captain was already there. After five minutes had passed Duncan appeared.

'This is not going to be easy', Duncan said anxiously to the two men.

'Look', said Alex, 'he sits in the café with the glass windows and watches the T.V., so if the Captain goes behind the wall opposite the building and keeps watch with the binoculars, until he falls asleep, then we will go round the rear and come in from the other side through the front door using the push bar. He won't see us'.

The Captain gave them the thumbs up and walked up the road towards the church from where Alex had come, before doubling back to take up position behind the wall in front of the distillery. He had the perfect view of Ian, the watchman, as he sat there watching the news and filling his face with crisps and sandwiches.

Unfortunately, it was a south westerly gale, and it was blowing right into Alex and Duncan.

'It's frickin' freezing', said Duncan, and as time went on the pair were becoming increasingly uncomfortable. It was almost fifty minutes later before the walkie talkie burst into life.

'Noodle nut loaf, the eagle has laid the golden egg'.

Duncan looked at Alex for clarification.

Alex picked up his receiver.

'Potato head. Can you repeat? Did you say the goose has lain the golden egg, over?'

'Nut loaf, it's an eagle remember, over'.

'Fuck me', said Alex, grabbing his friend's collar and pulling him to go round the side and rear of the building with him. Looking round from the other side of the building, Alex decided to check before they made their move to the Visitor Centre entrance.

'Potato head to Nut loaf, can you confirm there are no other birds in the vicinity, over'.

'Nut loaf, not at this time of night, over'.

'Copy that', said Alex and he waved to beckon Duncan to follow him.

Reaching the door with a brown façade at the entrance, he pressed the push bar and it clicked open, before proceeding on to and walking through the unlocked big white doors. Just like that and they were in.

'Where to now?' Alex whispered to his friend.

'The eagle is to the right', his friend replied.

'Forget the eagle', Alex insisted. 'Where is the whisky?'

'You mean the "While We Wait"?' whispered Duncan.

'Forget "While We Wait"', said Alex feeling really angry.

'Well, what are we here for then?' protested Duncan rather loudly.

'Shhh…the whisky barrels. You know the Ex-bourbon whisky casks', said Alex regaining his composure.

'Left, left', said his friend, pointing in that direction.

The door was open and surprisingly they found several unopened casks, marked 2017 on the barrel.

'We need to carefully roll it out the door', said Alex quietly. 'You open the door for me, and I will roll I quietly to the first door'.

It was quite heavy and made a thud against the wall when Alex started to roll it, as it wouldn't roll straight until he got the hang of it. They made it into the passageway and Duncan held the white door open as Alex successfully negotiated the barrel through it. But then they hit a snag.

The entrance door with the push bars on either side, was narrower and the barrel could not be rolled through it on its side. They needed to turn it upright and manoeuvre it out of the door by rotating it on its circumference.

Once they had got it through the door and on its side again, they managed to roll it down the drive, after the Captain had made a quick 360 degrees check of the surrounding area, and had given them the thumbs up to indicate that the coast was clear.

Once they were on the road, Big Duncan and he rolled and rolled the barrel along the road as hard as they could. But they used a little too much force and the barrel got away from them and they went too far, taking it down the road towards Home Farm, rather than up the side road to the Old Post Office where Duncan lived.

They retrieved it, but the wood was very slippery in the rain and much heavier to push back up the hill. But then they received a call on the walkie talkie.

'Nut Loaf here. There are other birds on the road. Repeat, there are other birds on the road'.

Reaching the old telephone exchange building, they hid behind it with the barrel. They did what they could to hold their breaths as footsteps could be heard approaching.

WHEN THE BOAT COMES IN

John and Christina MacLean had retired to bed after the news at ten, leaving their youngest son to close the fire down for the night.

As Christina lay in bed, she thought about how it was good in so many ways to have the family back together again, though she was concerned that Alex and Malcolm had come to blows. She hoped that with the tragic death of Fiona, Alex might be a bit more reflective of his behavior towards everyone.

She knew he had feelings for her, but for some reason she was convinced he was scared of their intensity, so instead he presented as this uncaring, alpha male type of character, in an attempt to block them out. Malcolm was very different, but he was uncharacteristically a little unbearable at the present time, as he placed his emotions on his sleeve. She hoped that the blossoming relationship with Janice, the community nurse, continued to develop, because if it didn't, she predicted stormy weather ahead.

'Wouldn't it be nice to see an island wedding', she remarked aloud but got no response from her husband.

'I said, wouldn't it be nice to see an island wedding?' she restated, and having received no response a second time she sat up in bed. Taking one look at her husband she realized that something was not right.

She shot out of bed.

'Malcolm', she shouted, 'come here!'

When Malcolm entered his parent's bedroom, something he rarely did, he found his mother standing at his father's bedside gently pushing on his shoulder. His father was sitting there, slightly slumped to the side. His eyes were rolling upwards under the eyelids, and he looked limp.

'Dad!' he shouted, and he and his mother just looked at one another despairingly.

'He's breathing', she reassured him in a shaky voice. 'Phone the surgery Malcolm', she instructed.

Malcolm went back to the sitting room and took the phone. It was a recorded message asking the caller to phone another number. He dialed it.

'Inverarish 660998', came the response. The voice was familiar.

'Hello', he replied, 'it's Malcolm…'

'Malcolm, it's nice to hear you but it's nearly midnight', said Janice a little exasperated, as it had been a long day. She had even phoned him earlier in the evening.

'Janice, it's my Dad', he fired off. Without stopping for breath, he quickly added, 'He's not saying anything and has fallen to one side. I'm sorry. The number told me to phone here, and as I was dialing it, I thought I know this number, I know this…'

She cut him off.

'Okay Malcolm, it's okay. Now is anyone with him just now?' she asked calmly.

'Yes, my Mum', he said.

'So, was he breathing, or is there anything more you can tell me?'

'Yes, yes, Mum said he was breathing, but his eyes look funny'.

'I'm going to drive over Malcolm, I'll be five, maybe ten minutes at the most'.

As Janice dressed quickly, she was anxious for Malcolm and the family. His father, John, was a tall man and was what you would call more of an old gentleman type of character, though he was quick witted too. For a moment she smiled to herself, as she asked herself just how much of the island's medical resources this family was taking up over the last few weeks. The only one she wouldn't have attended to was his mother.

Christina was relieved when John began to mutter a few, though, very unintelligible words.

'Shall I go and ask Alex to come? Malcolm asked, albeit reluctantly.

'Wait till the nurse comes', his mother said. 'We'll see what she says, and if we need him we'll call on him then'.

Now Janice drove quickly at the best of times, but it seemed that mother and son had barely finished their conversation, when they heard a knock at the door and Janice walked into the sitting room.

Malcolm met her in the lounge and she noticed how white he appeared. She stopped and spoke to him.

'Are you okay?' she asked.

'Aye', said Malcolm, 'but my Dad looks in a bad way'.

They went through to the bedroom at the end of the narrow passageway together.

'Mum…Janice', announced Malcolm.

Janice went over to the side of the bed.
She knelt down and took his father's arm, and took his pulse while studying her watch closely.

'Okay Mr. MacLean', she said, 'can you remember my name?'

He looked at her, or had the appearance of looking right through her.

'I want you to squeeze my hand', she said. And he did so, rather tight.
'No, the other one', she guided his other rather heavy hand onto hers, but he could not grasp it.

'When did this happen Mrs. MacLean?' she asked his wife.

'We went to bed sometime after ten and we were reading. I spoke to him just before the "Today in Parliament" programme, as he listens to it before the news and shipping forecast. But this time, he just didn't reply', she sniveled.

'It's okay', Janice reassured her with a comforting touch on her shoulder. She turned to her husband again.
'I'm just going to take your blood pressure', she informed him.

After the armband had squeezed the life out of John's arm, and as Janice read the gauge on the appliance, rather calmly he said with tiredness in his voice,

'That was rather tight dear'.

'Oh, you're back in the land of the living with us!' laughed Janice.

'Oh, my dear!' exclaimed Christina, and Malcolm looked relieved.

'Was I away?' joked John in a quieter than normal voice.

'You just wanted to get me out my bed', joked Janice. 'I just need to do a few more tests with you if you don't mind'.

John raised his hand, either in a resigned but consensual manner, or in a whatever will be form of response. Janice spent another five minutes testing his responses and recognition of what he was seeing. His strength had returned to his right hand and arm.

As she went to leave the house and return home for her beauty sleep, and after making a telephone call, she told Christina that she thought, but did not know as she was not a Doctor, that her husband had possibly had a trans-ischaemic attack. The G.P. on-call she had spoken to in Portree, had agreed however, that this was likely from the symptoms they described.

'And what's that?' asked his wife.

'It's like a mini-stroke', Janice informed her. 'I'm going to leave you with an Aspirin for him to take and I'd like him to see the Doctor when they are next over. I thought for a minute we might have to contact the ferry and ask them if they could take him over to the hospital in Portree, but when he regained his physical functions, or abilities, I think, and so does the Doctor, that moving him now would be of little help'.

'Yes', said Christina, 'I'll make sure he's at the surgery first thing when it opens again next week'.

'They'll probably put him on some medication', Janice advised, 'and hopefully that will be him for a good while. Here's hoping anyway. Any more problems overnight, just call me'.

Malcolm walked her out to the car.

'You okay now?' she asked him.

He cuddled her, quite intensely, so much so that she thought her ribs might snap at any second.
She looked around as she was technically on duty, and then kissed him.

When he went back indoors, his mother was just washing the glass with which she had given her husband some water to take with the aspirin.

'Thank goodness for your Janice', said his mother.

'Do you want me to go and tell Alex just now?' he asked her.

'No', she said, 'I think he's got enough on his plate just now'.

A PAIN IN THE BUTT

It felt like a good five minutes had elapsed as they held their breath. And just as they were about to sharply exhale, they rose ten feet in the air as a face suddenly appeared from around the corner and looked directly at them.

'All clear', said the Captain.

'Fuck me!' Alex exclaimed, and Duncan held his heart as if he was about to sustain an attack.

'Come on', said Alex regaining his composure, 'let's get it up to the back garden'.

The three of them rolled the oak barrel, and, without too much of a problem or any more moments of crisis befalling them, managed to get it in by the side gate, up the back of the house and onto the grass. It was much harder to push, but they rolled it up beside where the new 250 litre water butt sat, beside the shed, which Duncan had been busy converting into an outdoor pub.

'Aye we need to roll it onto the higher ground, so that it's higher', the Captain instructed.

'Higher than what?' Duncan queried.

'The butt', said the Captain.

Duncan waited but there was no clarification.

'But what?' he asked.

'The barrel is above the butt', explained the Captain.

'The barrel is above *the what?*' asked Duncan getting a bit fed up at the Captain's inability to explain himself.
Maybe Alex was right, he thought, and the Captain wasn't up to the job.

'The butt… the water butt! The barrel has to be higher than the water butt', said the Captain animated and increasingly exasperated.

Alex just stood there and wondered for a moment how the ferry was still in one piece, or for that matter, the passengers and their vehicles.

They rolled the barrel up the slight incline and onto the concreted ground on which the shed cum pub was built, and left it sitting horizontally on the ground. The Captain jumped down and took the lid off the butt, before climbing up to the concreted area again. He then took a holdall from the wooden structure which he had brought round earlier in the evening, which contained about 10 empty whisky bottles and a hammer, and also a plastic sleeve with a length of new hose in it. He took the hammer, and as if he did it for a living, tapped the round opening plug of the whisky barrel until it dislodged. He spent a few moments inserting the hose carefully, before jumping down onto the grass again, and picking up the other end of the hose, he sucked on it at the butt end, and then the whisky started to flow from one receptacle into the other.

It was not a quick job, and they had to turn the barrel upright, and then hold it up in the air eventually, to get every last drop from the wooden barrel to drain into the very full water butt.

As the last drips plopped into the butt, and as the captain secured its lid, he jumped up on to the concreted area again. Alex thought he was going to retrieve the hose and seal off the barrel, but instead he grabbed his holdall, jumped down onto the grass, took out two bottles and opened the tap of the water butt. It quickly filled the first bottle with whisky and he was soon filling the second.

'Hold on', said Alex. 'We need to get this back before fat Ian wakens up'.

'Plenty time laddie' said the Captain, before adding in delight with a hearty laugh, 'there is enough for one hundred bottles each here. This is what they must mean by cask share!' He took more than a mouthful of the amber coloured liquid, before turning to Duncan. 'Taste the peat in that, will you?'

He handed Duncan the bottle and he too downed somewhat more than a mouthful.

'Oh, come on guys', said Alex getting anxious that the pair would get intoxicated before the job was done. 'We need to get this back, or else they will suspect it's been stolen'.

'Hold on a minute, just let me finish filling this one will you?' said the Captain a little irate.

Duncan took another swig and looking at Alex noted the look of derision on his face.

'Okay Potato head', laughed Duncan. 'Ready'.

Needless to say, replacing the wooden plug on an empty barrel and rolling it back, was a much easier task than when they removed it.

The Captain got into position behind the wall with a pair of binoculars in one hand, and holding what was now a half empty bottle of whisky in the other, he emptied the remaining contents into his mouth. Alex and Duncan got to the entrance to the complex and got the thumbs up from the Captain. It was easy manoeuvering the barrel through the narrower entrance door than when they had tried to exit with it when full, and the returning of the empty barrel which looked discoloured and wet, posed no difficulty.

As they dropped off the barrel the walkie talkie crackled but the message was incoherent. Alex and Duncan were approaching the white door, with only one door remaining to get through.

'Repeat that Nut Loaf, over', said Alex, very quietly into his handset.

The walkie talkie crackled into life and the voice was much clearer.

'*Goosey goosey gander, Whither shall I wander? Upstairs and downstairs And in my lady's chamber*'.

Alex was unsure what was meant, so he tried again.

'Is the goose on the move?'

There was a short period of silence, and then the response came.

The stairs went crack; He nearly broke his back. And all the little ducks went, Quack, quack, QUACK'.

'Let's just get the fuck out of here!' exclaimed Alex.

Whether it was the much louder quack at the end of the message that roused fat Ian, or else it actually was a signal that he was already on the move, neither of them really knew, but as they made their speedy exit through the doors, they could hear footsteps approaching from the cafeteria area, so they ran as fast as they could down the path. Noticing the Captain was now lying on the road, rather than behind the wall, they took an arm each and draping one each over their shoulders, headed back with him to the Old Post Office.

As they reached the back garden, they threw themselves in exhaustion onto the wet ground, before breaking into uncontrollable laughter.

It was an hour before sunrise when Alex finally made it home exhausted, having taken some refreshment before his journey home.
He opened the pod, and threw himself face down on the camp bed.

When he awoke some hours later, he didn't expect his mother to be standing over him in the Pod holding a lunch box. She looked at the mess of the small living area and the remains of the food items he had consumed from previous days that he had not discarded.

'Mother', he groaned. 'You startled me'.

As he wiped his eyes as the light seemed to pierce through them like a burning laser, she started to recount to him the events of the previous night. He did not reciprocate with an account of his night's exploits, but smelling the alcohol, his mother assumed he had been drowning his sorrows.

'Fiona's funeral is on Monday Alex', she said. 'I know it's hard that no-one can go except for her Mum, and the extended family, but try not and console yourself through alcohol'.

When she finally left him amidst his swill, Alex was more consumed with thoughts about his father's health. As the patriarch, everything had centred around him throughout all his years growing up, and what he was doing on the croft.

How many times in his childhood had he heard the words, 'we can't do this as your Dad's got to attend to', whatever the task was, that was needing to be attended to might be.

THE UNOFFICAL WAKE

That next morning, John MacLean had wakened to also find his wife standing over him at the side of his bed. He remembered having the feeling of an intense headache and falling ill the previous night. At the time he was having his attack, or afterwards, all he could think of was wanting to get out of the situation he had found himself in, so that he could show his wife where the copy of his will was, and the paper with all the bank details on it, in case he never made it through.

He felt tired on awakening and he was aware he was not focusing as well as he normally did.

'Yes, the young nurse, Janice, came over', she told him, but he recollected very little from the previous night.

'I meant to tell you the copy of the will is in my box', he said, 'with a note of all the bank accounts and pin numbers'.

'What are you telling me that for John?'

She laughed feeling frightened but not wanting to show it.

'You're not getting away from me that easily', she said.

At dinner that evening at five o'clock, everyone was gathered around the table, and there was little evidence of hostility between the two brothers on show. Some of that might have been due to Alex too still feeling the worse for wear, but as a mealtime in the MacLean household, on this occasion it was an amicable affair.

Indeed, over the next few days, mealtimes seemed to pass by without any sarcastic interchanges occurring, and John although feeling less sure of himself, seemed to be making a good recovery.

For Malcolm, the added bonus, if in fact you could call it a bonus, was that Janice called in the next day to check on her patient. This was particularly welcome, not just because she was attending to his father, but with Mrs. MacKay's leg healing, the opportunities for clandestine meetings during Janice's working hours were few and far between. The visit, or visits as it turned out to be, legitimized their meeting, though much interaction was from behind face masks.

Alex managed to clean up the Glamping Pod and spent the remainder of that week in study and detoxification. His head had fair taken a pounding for a few days and it was sensitive to the light. He had also decided to stay away from Duncan's for a few days to let things die down a bit and to avoid rousing suspicions by visiting there too much in the aftermath. But he was anxious to hear if there had been any news of the raid on the distillery. Having heard absolutely nothing, he determined that in this instance, no news was in fact good news.

He remained blissfully unaware that Ian, the watchman, had in fact been disturbed from his sleep by a noise, on the night of the raid. But having reached the front door of the distillery, he pressed the push bar to open it, but was pushed back by a strong gust of wind. So, he had reasoned the noise that had disturbed him had just been caused by the gale, thought little more of it, and had soon returned to his slumber.

The following Wednesday, having allowed a week to pass, Alex took the lift into Inverarish in the morning with his parents, who were going to the surgery for the first doctor's appointment at nine.
He walked down to the pier to await the first ferry from Sconser that was due in around the same time.

'How's it going Duncan?' he asked when the last car had cleared the deck.

'All good good, man', his friend replied while the Captain waved to him from the bridge which he acknowledged returning the gesture.

'Any word?' he asked.

'Word about what?' asked Duncan.

'About, you know…?' There was still no response, so he added quickly, 'the whisky'.

'It's bloody good stuff man!' Duncan exclaimed. 'The Captain took another ten bottles this morning', he said leading him to a small seat like box at the side of the car deck. He discreetly opened it and there lying on some rope, was ten bottles of whisky.

Alex looked up at his friend a little surprised.

'It can get quite boring on the ferry sometimes', he informed, 'going up and down the Sound all day'.

Alex brought back to mind his original query and asked more explicitly, 'Have you heard any word about the whisky going missing?'

'It's in the water butt!' Duncan exclaimed in disbelief.

'Shhh', said his friend although no-one was around to hear. He composed himself and tried again. 'Has anyone said about the whisky going missing from the distillery?'

'Not a word, not a sheep's bleat', said Duncan which served to re-assure him. 'Come up for lunch at mid-day', offered Duncan. 'I change over after the next ferry run so I'm off now till next Monday'.

'Okay, sure', Alex replied. 'I'll see you up there. You do know Fiona's funeral starts at twelve?' he said.

'Aye, you'll see the cortege', Duncan informed, 'from the window'.

The Old Post Office where Duncan lived was at the bottom of the road that led up to the cemetery.

The Doctor examined his patient thoroughly, and undertook weight, blood pressure, heart rate and blood tests.

'The results won't be back until the middle of the week', she said referring to the blood samples she had taken, 'but I think the nurse and the Doctor the other night were probably spot on when they said you had had a trans-ischaemic attack. I think I'll put you on some blood pressure tablets and get you take some aspirin each morning John', she said. 'Maybe just treat this as a warning shot for the moment. You are a tall man, but you could maybe change your diet a little and eat some more greens'.

'Oh, don't worry', said his wife, 'I have already changed his diet. It's salad every day for lunch'. John rolled his eyebrows which the Doctor noticed. She laughed.

'Well done Christina', she exclaimed in delight.

Alex called into the Community Store and Post Office while he was in the main village. He also knew if there had been any hint of gossip about even a biscuit going missing from the distillery, he would be sure to hear about it in the shop.
But when he got there, he sensed there was an atmosphere, a tension that hung around in the air in the shop.
James, the shopkeeper, was in a sombre mood.

Alex became suspicious that maybe someone knew something was amiss at the distillery, so he tried to engage James in conversation to find out what was wrong.

'I'm going up your way if you want a lift home?' James the shopkeeper suddenly invited.

'Aye sure', said Alex, thinking this would let him probe some more.
'What are you going up to mine for?' he asked.

'I'm dropping off some groceries to a few people who can't get down to the shop' he informed.

The car journey was illuminating, if only for the fact that there was no news whatsoever of the missing whisky.
Like most of the people on the island that day, James was just feeling sad at the death of Fiona, with her funeral being imminent. He expressed his sympathies to Alex, and went on to lament the fact that it was only the close family that were being allowed to attend the funeral.

'You can always stand by the roadside and clap', he said, trying to offer Alex some consolation. 'That's being respectful', he suggested.

James dropped him off at the gate to the Potato field, and he walked down to the pod with a smile on his face. After dropping off some cigarettes and chocolate, as he had never intended to buy anything but felt obliged, as a down payment for the 'good craic' as some of the older people in the village would call it, he walked up to the croft house.

His mother gave him the news of his father's appointment, and asked if he wanted to stay on for lunch, but he reminded her it was Fiona's funeral and he was going to Duncan's for lunch.

He got to the pier for the arrival of the incoming ferry, which was five minutes late, and which he was grateful for, as he didn't really want to be walking up the road to Duncan's just before the funeral was scheduled to start, in case he passed any of the extended family on their way there.

'Freedom!' shouted Duncan as he disembarked and waved an exaggerated farewell to the Captain, and deckhand who had taken over from him for the four days.

When they got to the house, Alex noted the golden eagle hovering high up in the sky being pursued he thought by two crows. He ducked at the last moment, managing to avoid the small entrance.

Duncan offered his friend some chips and to fry up some sausages.

'Aye eh...okay', said Alex thinking twice about it, and walked out into the back garden.

The water butt was gone.
He returned inside looking alarmed.

'Where's your butt?' he asked his portly friend.

Duncan reached into his pocket and threw him a small key.

'You'll need it for the padlock. Go and have a look', he grinned.

Alex walked up to the garden shed and loosened the padlock. When he opened the door. His head recoiled slightly and he grinned from ear.

'Fuck me Deep Fry!' he exclaimed.

Behind a home-made counter top were a row of shelves on the wall, and on them were about a dozen bottles of whisky. Beside those, sat some cans of cider and some bottled lager. Hanging up and attached to the wall, were two larger bottles of whisky attached to some optics. He looked behind the counter and found the water butt.

In front of the counter and a ledge for sitting a glass or can on, sat three stools for sitting on. Duncan had even set up a television on a bracket and DVD player in a corner shelf, and an old boom box sat on the counter. It was a home garden pub, and asides from Raasay House which was currently closed, was the only working pub on the island. He had even put some whisky glasses, beer glasses and an ashtray in it.

'Bloody good, bloody good, eh?' said his friend popping his head in the door behind him.

'Bloody marvelous!' said Alex looking around in wonder like a dazzled child in some Santa's Grotto at Christmas.

'I think we should have one now before we eat', suggested Duncan.

'I don't know, it's maybe a bit …,' said Alex.

'For Fiona?' said his friend.

'Aye, to Fiona', said Alex and Duncan went behind the bar and put two glasses up to the optics. Pub measures although they were, he put five measures in each glass.

'Slainte!' he said lifting his glass, as did Alex, and the amber liquid was gone.

'I think we should go out to the roadside', said Alex, 'and watch the cortege go by when they come down the road from the church'.

'Aye, you're right', said Duncan, 'one for the road'.

He took both glasses and poured out an equally liberal measure as before.

'To Fiona', said Alex nodding seriously.

'To Fiona', said Duncan.

Both men walked down the side of the house and stood by the road. He had only had two glasses but Alex could feel the effects already of his pre-lunch indulgences. Duncan did too, and realizing his temporary amnesia, nipped back inside to switch off the frying pan.

As Alex walked down to the corner of the road, he noticed what he mistook to be a procession of people walking up the road towards him. But in fact, they were stationary. He realized that people from all over the island had come to line the route to pay their respects to one of their own. Then came a loud noise which made him feel temporarily disorientated, as he could not process where it was coming from, or what was going on.

Big Duncan rejoined him.

'Listen, they're clapping', he said to Alex and joined in.

It was not long before the small solemn procession drove past the two men. Alex noticed in the hearse there were two wreaths, one spelt out the word

DAUGHTER

and another

BEST FRIEND

Around the same time a hundred and eighty miles away in the suburbs of Glasgow, Mary was lighting a candle and saying a prayer. She crossed herself as she thought about her closest friend.

Alex started clapping too. Fiona's mother looked at Alex either in acknowledgment of the act of respect, or just straight through him, without any visible emotion showing in her face. The cortege of three cars drove up the single-track road towards the cemetery.

Alex stood there, pensive, as the cortege disappeared from view.

Duncan had already gone indoors and when Alex found him, he was putting eight black sausages on the two plates.

'I turned the wrong ring on the cooker off' he said holding one up in the air.

It resembled a charred log as it left an ash residue on his fingers when he put it back on his plate. 'But the chips are good' he offered by way of consolation.

'Shall we go down the pub?' he asked his friend.

'Aye', said Alex, 'to the pub it is'.

Once they went back into the garden pub with their plates in hand, his friend retrieved a music tape from behind the counter top and put it in the boom box.
As he looked and tried to cut the sausage, to a musical backing from the late 60's, its sombre tone struck him. It was like a dirge.

'Another?' said his friend holding his glass up to the optic, having sensed Alex had gone quiet.

'Go on', said Alex as he lost count of how many presses of the optic Duncan made.

'That's my man', he shouted with glee as he tried to lighten the mood.

But as the Minister had said at Fiona's funeral,

'For everything there is a season, and a time for every matter under heaven: a time to be born, and a time to die…a time to weep, and a time to laugh; a time to mourn and a time to dance…a time to keep silence, and a time to speak'.

He did not wish to speak at this moment but instead to mourn, and the alcohol only served to exacerbate that feeling. He was soon drinking another.

Needless to say, Duncan needed little encouragement, and time got the better of them.

They were surprised when the Captain appeared, with his holdall, and another ten empty bottles for filling, not because of his appearance for that purpose, but more so because Duncan knew they wouldn't be finished the evening run till after half past six in the evening. They had been drinking for six hours and he had not noticed that his friend was actually sleeping, slumped over the counter on his stool.

'Only another twenty more to fill and I'll have had my fair share', he declared as he carefully put the holdall over his shoulder and walked off. Duncan said nothing, nor did he follow him, as he was not able to rise from the stool either.

It was now nearer seven in the evening and Christina MacLean was worried about her son. She knew he was the elder and that things leading up to her husband's illness had been a bit fractious of late, but he would always make the effort to be at the dinner table at five.

'I'll take a drive into the village and see if I see him, if you want?' said John MacLean.

'No', she said, 'I think I'll drive in myself if you don't mind', she replied.

Christina knew that he had gone to Duncan's for lunch, and knowing Duncan from when he was very young, he knew how the two would egg each other on and get into bother before having the wisdom to call a halt to whatever they were doing.

With Fiona's death and the funeral being held today, she was in little doubt they would have secured something with which to mark the occasion. She had turned a blind eye to her eldest son's drinking and smoking, and she was in no doubt smoking of other substances too, as she just put it down to the experience of teenage years. But his attitude to women caused her some concern, and although she was sure it was just a façade to block out his true feelings, she sometimes wondered if it affected his behaviour towards other woman. His attitude laterally to Fiona she felt, was evidence of that, and she suspected deep down he was now regretting that and was struggling as a result to manage his deeper feelings.

As she drove towards the old Post Office, she was not too sure what she would find, but she was pretty certain it would not be good. When she reached the house, she was surprised to find the two young men in the sitting room, clearly trying to sober up with copious amounts of coffee.

'Mother', he simply said with a long-drawn face.

'Come on', she said, 'let's go in the car'.

Alex rose, and stuck his thumb in the air to acknowledge his friend who tried to act proper in the presence of his friend's mother.

'Do come again', he said in an attempt at a posh voice.

Alex stumbled into the passenger's seat in the car, having suggested he just take a seat in the back instead. But his mother would have none of it and she had mumbled something at him about how he needed to be in the front of the vehicle.

He was unsure, but he was certain this was not the road home, passing the lochan and the Kayaks that lay on the verge, on the right-hand side of the road. By the time he was able to think coherently enough to ask where they were going, they had arrived.

'Come on,' said his mother as she opened her door and climbed out.

He fumbled to release his seat belt and eventually followed her. When he got out the car, he was greeted by a sign about a stone in remembrance of two prisoners of war, and then looking past it and through the iron railings, he realised he was at the graveyard.

'Oh mother', he moaned, 'why did you bring me here? Of all days…'

'Come on' she said grasping his hand, as if he was going to school with her again for his very first day, 'we need to pay our respects'.

'But I've done that already', he protested, but she pulled him along behind him.

As they stood by the graveside, his mother opened her handbag and took out some freshly cut flowers. She had cut them from one of the planters which she cultivated outside the croft house front door.

'May God Bless you and may you rest in peace my dear', she said as she knelt down and placed them on the ground beside the freshly dug grave. 'Do you not want to say anything Alex?' she asked looking at him.

'Do I have to…Mum?' he asked and started to cry.

She held him consoling him, which was the first time she had done so from the time when he was in the Primary School, maybe some sixteen years ago now.

'It didn't work out', he sobbed. 'We wanted very different things. I didn't want what Fiona wanted Mum'. There was a period of silence, and then he blurted out, 'I just wanted to be all I can be'.

'I know dear', she consoled, 'but you know, life is sometimes a bit of give and take. It's not always about ourselves and meeting our own needs, but sometimes it's about what we can do for others. That's what often brings us true happiness in the end'.

He was gaining sobriety with each moment they spent by the graveside, and he felt the desperate urge to leave.

'Can we go now Mum, please?' he asked his pleading visible in his eyes.

She didn't move.

'I did love her Mum, I did you know', he cried.

'I know' she said, 'but unfortunately it's only when people are gone that we truly find out who we really love'.

She took his hand and they walked back to the car.

The drive home was a silent affair and she stopped and let him out at the gate. She sat there and watched him as he slowly walked down the field towards the glamping pod. He stumbled on the rough terrain, but this was probably due to being worse the wear through drink.
She was not going make excuses for his behaviour to herself any longer, and pretend it was something it was not. She was his mother, and if there was little else she could do for him at this stage in his life, then the very least she could do, she reasoned, would be to instill in him an understanding that women have feelings, and a right to be treated with respect too.

SUSPICIONS

About a week had passed and mealtimes had been rather subdued and routine affairs. Alex felt as if everything was still going on as normal amidst the death of Fiona, which left him feeling as very discordant, and slightly out of step with everything that was going around him. He had an assignment that was due in and then some exams to sit online, which helped divert his mind from other things.

That's why it was with some surprise that the following Wednesday, when Malcolm had agreed to drive his father down to the surgery for his follow-up appointment, which he was quick to volunteer for, as Janice was the nurse on-call that week in the surgery and which gave them an increasingly rare opportunity to spend some limited time together amidst the lockdown, that he was surprised to see his brother in the village.

Having taken his father back home, he returned to the village, and coming in via the high road past Raasay House and on down towards the Community Stores, he was surprised to see Alex walking down in the direction of the park carrying a carrier bag.
With his curiosity perked, he parked the car beside the shop and hastened down towards the bridge near the Heritage Centre building, but keeping his distance.
When he rounded the corner opposite the row of houses, he saw his brother walking past the park in the direction of the Free Presbyterian Church.

As he walked at a distance behind, he was surprised to see his brother did not continue up towards the Church and onto Raasay House, which is one way of walking to their home, but instead he headed towards the school and into the surgery.

Once he knew his brother had gone into the surgery, where he had only been himself less than an hour ago, he ran towards the new community hall and stood near the driveway to get a good view of the surgery road end.

Some time passed causing Malcolm increasing angst, and it was some ten to fifteen minutes later before his older brother emerged. He watched him walk slowly up towards the Church in the opposite direction from where he hid.

When he was out of view, Malcolm emerged from his hiding place and walked slowly back towards the shop. He thought about all the reasons his brother could be there. Maybe he needed to have the strips removed from his forehead, but that was a nonsense, as they were long gone and he never needed his removed as they fell off naturally. Maybe he needed to pick up a prescription for his father, but that just wasn't possible as he had just taken him to the surgery himself. Maybe it was his worst fear after all which he didn't want to acknowledge, but now he had to start thinking it.

Alex walked past the Old Post Office and headed for Oscaig, while his brother reached his car and having not even given a moment's thought as to why he had come to the shop in the first place, he started to drive home. As he reached the sign for the Fearns and the North Pole, he realized that he had forgotten to pick up the paper and the box of aspirin, so he drove back down to the shop for a second time.

When he was in the shop, James the shopkeeper said to him,
'You just missed your brother Malcolm; he was here not that long ago'.

'Oh', said Malcolm, half feigning surprise. 'Shame I missed him' he said dryly.

'He said he needed to go and see someone at the surgery', said James. 'You'll maybe get him there'.

Malcolm just stood there. That was it confirmed.

Alex passed the potato field and went on past the Croft House. he walked on until he came to Jean MacKay's house, and stood at the door knocking.

Jean, whose leg was much better which meant she had regained sufficient mobility to manage independently around her house, came to the door. She was surprised to see Alex MacLean there. She had often babysat for the MacLeans, on the rare occasion the boys' parents had a social event to attend, and it had been probably a few years since she had spoken directly to Alex.

'Alex', she said not masking her surprise.

'Mrs. MacKay', he replied holding a bag of groceries out towards her. 'I was in James' shop', he explained, 'and he said he was needing to come up and drop these off for you. I know he was having trouble getting out, so if you don't mind, I said I was going home so I could drop them off'.

'Oh, that's very kind of you dear', she said.

'Oh', said Alex nearly forgetting something. He pulled out a small bag from his jacket pocket. 'He asked me to collect these and bring them to you at the same time', he said passing over the small bag.

'Perfect', she said, 'I was waiting on these'. She turned to go back indoors but instead turned around again to speak to Alex who was also about to turn around and leave.
'Would you like a cup of tea?' she offered with a smile.

Now normally Alex would protest that older people just talk about the war and particularly Raasay folk just talk about events from the distant pass that would bore the hind legs of a donkey, so his instinct was to reject the offer.

'Eh thank you very much, but…', he said, before adding, 'I don't want to put you at any risk with this virus'.

'I think we can visit another household now', she said, 'and I will not be seeing anyone else from any other households, so I have no problem'.

Alex stood there and there was a short period of silence.

'Then I have no problem too', he said.

She stood aside and let him come in.

When Malcolm returned home, he appeared a little out of sorts.
He gave his father the paper and the box of aspirin. His mother taking the box of aspirin from his father's hand said, 'I'll take those thank you', and within a minute one tablet was dispensed to his father with some water.

'It's good the Doctor said that to you dear', she said to his father.

'Yes, I guess so', he said. 'They are so much cheaper at the shop'.

'It also saves a trip each Wednesday to the surgery', his mother said. 'But you would have gone, wouldn't you, son?' she smiled towards Malcolm.

'I think Alex would prefer to', he retorted and walked out.

John MacLean spluttered in his tea, half laughing and half taken aback at his son's abrupt response and equally as sharp exit.

'What did I say?' Christina said with a look of surprise in her face.

Unaware that he was the main feature of the conversation elsewhere, Alex listened to Jeannie talk at some length about how the problem with her leg had prevented her from attending to a whole range of things.

'You know your brother was coming for a while to put on my fire when it was really bad', she informed him.

'Aye, he's got a big heart', said Alex. 'I sometimes wish I could be a bit more like him myself'.
Alex laughed, completely oblivious to the fact that his brother was far from feeling kind hearted towards him at this moment in time.

'What do you mean dear?' asked Jean MacKay, surprised to hear the older brother engage in a rare moment of self-reflection.

'I suppose', thought Alex in some deep thought. He then rejoined the conversation. 'Thanks for the tea, Mrs. MacKay'.

'Jeannie', she said suggesting he call her that.

'If there's anything else you need', he said, 'just let me know'.

'Well', she said and she started to talk some more.

MORE SUSPICIONS

The following week when he went to collect Jeannie MacKay's prescription and groceries, Alex decided to take a detour on the road home, and headed down the pier instead to see Duncan who was just about to finish work before heading up the road for lunch.

As they walked together up towards the Old Post Office, Duncan recounted how the Captain had been temporarily suspended from duty further to an investigation.

'Was he drinking on duty?' asked Alex innocently.

'No, it wasn't that', informed Duncan. 'There was a complaint about his behavior towards the passengers. I think it was those two men who tried to come over last month. You remember?'

'Aye', said Alex emphatically. 'But he never did anything. They should never have come over in the first place. They even ended up at my mother's door looking for accommodation'.

'Aye', responded Duncan 'You know I remember we took them back on the evening ferry that night, and the slimy bastards were as nice as ninepence to us. In fact, they never even saw the captain to speak to on the return leg'.

'That's so wrong', exclaimed Alex.

Unusually Alex did not join his friend for lunch on this occasion, or for some of the amber liquid which was depleting fast, but instead walked on up the road towards home. Once again, instead of turning off at the Potato field, he called in at Jean MacKay's and handed in her groceries to her. On this occasion he did not however, go in for tea, despite her offer, but instead continued to walk up the road towards Glame.

When Malcolm called at the surgery to collect his father's blood pressure medication, he met with Janice in the car park beside the houses. Wearing a face mask, she sat in the car and they talked for a while. She found him a bit distant and wondered if he was a bit worried about his father. Unfortunately, she did not have the time to pursue the matter with him, as she had been asked to do a priority visit, so when she got out the car she jumped in her Fiesta and sped off down the road towards Suisnish.

When he went into the surgery he asked for his father's medication and was surprised at the response he got.

'I'm surprised your brother didn't ask for it when he was in earlier', the receptionist informed him.

Malcolm was silent, for Janice had made no mention of it either.

When Alex reached Holoman after about forty minutes of walking, he saw an older man in the field. He waved to him and he waved back. Alex walked over the rough ground and greeted the man.

'So, Stuart, this is where all the action is taking place I believe', he said.

'Aye', said Stuart who was probably in his late sixties by now. 'If you go over there', he said pointing to where his satchel lay on the ground with a flask, you'll get one there.

Alex walked over to the bag and saw a wooden shafted spade on the ground, which matched the one the older man was working with.

'Where do you want me?' Alex asked.

'Just work this bank with me', said Stuart. 'I'll do one and you do the next'.

'It's years since I did this', said Alex watching the technique of his older mentor. But in no time, he was soon digging the spade in and bringing out the blackened peat from the soil like slices of cake. The digging he did not mind. It was later in the season when they were drier and gathered that was the real back breaking stuff, but at least he would have helped cut them and Jeannie would have her own supply for later in the year.

The two men worked solidly for around four hours, only stopping once for a fifteen minutes break from the flask that Stuart had brought with him onto the hillside.

'Do you not want a lift back down the road? he asked. Alex looked at his phone. It was half past four.

'No, I've got a call I need to make', Alex informed. 'I'll probably just take my time walking back and do it at the same time'.

"Please yourself', said Stuart, 'the offer is always there'.

'Cheers', said Alex, retrieving his jacket as he bid farewell to his digging partner.

'Till the next time!' he shouted back, as he walked down the hill.

The reception was good as he made his call.

'Caledonian MacBrayne', came the voice on the other end.

'Yes, hello. My name is Alex MacLean. I was wondering if I could speak to someone in the customer complaints section, please?' he asked.

'I'm sorry Mr. MacLean, but Mr. Brown who normally handles customer care is actually away to Skye this week'

'Oh', said Alex, 'that's a shame. I need to speak to him about the Captain on the Sconser to Raasay ferry'. There was a short silence.

'Oh, well if you leave me your number Mr. MacLean', the receptionist replied, 'I could ask him to give you a call when he gets back in touch'.

'Yes', said Alex, 'that would be fine thanks'.
He proceeded to give her his number.

When he arrived at the dinner table a few minutes before five o'clock, he was conscious that there was an atmosphere at the dinner table. Christina MacLean was also aware of the tense atmosphere but did not know what the undercurrent to it all was. Dinner passed off without incident, things seemed to carry on as normal, but something was jarring and she wasn't quite sure what it was.

GUILTY UNTIL PROVEN INNOCENT

That night as he walked back to his Pod, Alex noticed that he had missed a call from a Greenock number.

'Damn', he muttered to himself as he walked down to the potato field. At least the reception is better down here than at the house, he thought.

He rose early and spent the early morning putting the finishing touches to his assignment, once he had ironed out the stiffness in his back. He did several stretches, and he smiled as he thought of himself as a yogic hermit, practicing his stretches out on his front porch in the presence of mother nature.

When nine o'clock came he phoned the missed call on his mobile phone, and was told he would get a call in response to his query at ten o'clock, and was asked whether or not he would be available to take it.

'Of course', he responded a little put out, as it was he who had called in the first place.

He returned to his computer and looked at the log in details for the deferred mid-May examination. Once he logged on and completed it, it would all be over, providing he passed it that was. He would hopefully walk out with the teaching diploma to complement his degree in physics, and the prospect of a science teacher's post at one of the schools beckoned. Mind you, he thought, will there even be schools recruiting for the new academic year if this lockdown goes on much further?

Alex was also unsure if the idea of being a science teacher in a secondary school was still as an exciting prospect as it once was. Why is it, he thought, that when you study something, it never turns out to be as appealing as the thought of doing it was?

As he sat there contemplating life, he looked out of the glamping pod window and saw his brother roaming the field studying the development of the potato crop.
They had had that fight which he sorely regretted and things seemed to be returning to a more harmonious state between them, but in the last few weeks he had found the silences had all reappeared and he wasn't too sure what he had done, or if even it was himself that had done anything. Alex was about to go out and walk over and speak to him, but the phone rang just as he was about to go outdoors.

'Yes, yes that's me', he said.

Malcolm plodded the field, restless, agitated, and he wondered if he should confront his brother. Again, he decided the better of it, as he did not want it to end up in a fight again and he did not want to upset his mother and father, particularly given his father's high blood pressure. When they were young they were used to tip-toeing around him and accommodating the crofting lifestyle he was committed to, but now there was an even greater need to ensure he was not overburdened with anything.

'Look I know', said Alex emphatically into his phone. 'Social distancing or no social distancing, I was there'.

Maybe I'm just over-reacting, thought Malcolm. Remembering what his father had said to him, he decided to give him one more chance and returned home.

'What?' said Alex in disgust, continuing his conversation with the person on the other end of the phone. 'Is a person now guilty before they are proven innocent, is that what you are saying?'

When Malcolm reached the Croft house, he went in and sat down to breakfast. He noted his father was a bit chirpier than he had seen him of late. Christina MacLean had also noticed the same and both she and her son nodded at one another in recognition of the fact, when her husband was getting animated at something one of the politicians had said on the T.V.

'Silly bugger!' he had exclaimed, and they both laughed. His father thought they too were laughing at the politician. 'How can they defend that?' he cried again in derision of what was being said. 'I'll tell you this', he carried on conducting the conversation with himself, 'if they expect people to follow the rules after that, they're living in dreamland'.

'You're feeling rather animated about that, aren't you dear?' said his wife sitting down.

'Well, no wonder Christina', he said giving her her name, which he only really ever did when he was wanting to make what he felt was an important point. 'It's an open and shut case', he concluded.

'Well maybe he was just doing what he thought was right', she suggested, not too aware of the finite detail of the situation being talked about.

'I'm pretty sure he knew what he was doing dear', he said. The way he used the word 'dear' sometimes irked her a little, as it wasn't said in a soothing sort of way, but had a more accusatory tone to it.

'Well, we're all innocent until proven guilty', she asserted and rose up from her chair so as not to cause an argument and her husband undue stress. He continued the discussion with himself.

It was later that morning after the phone call that Alex decided the time had come to log on and take that examination. For the next three hours he applied himself to the task at hand. He was glad that as a result of the pandemic the examination had to be undertaken online, and although the connection sometimes caused his laptop camera to freeze on occasions, the camera being a requirement to ensure there was no cheating, he was able to type much faster than he could write so there would be no issues about handwriting that could not be read by the markers.

To mark the occasion, and now that it was early afternoon, Alex decided to go and see Duncan to celebrate. As he walked down the road feeling quite contended with himself, he was thinking about whether the diploma came with a grading. He was averaging around 62 per cent for the subjects taken so far, and if he could come close to that again that would surely fall into the classification of a Merit, he thought.

As he calculated all the ramifications in his head, he was oblivious to the fact that his younger brother was trailing him at a distance. When he reached Duncan's house, Alex knocked on the door and then walked up the side path when he got no answer.

Sure enough when he got there, he found Duncan in the pub, but he had company.

Having watched his brother progress no further than his friend's house, Malcolm started to walk back home and castigated himself with the thought that he really had to give his brother another chance.

'Slainte mhath ya bastard!' exclaimed the Captain when Alex opened the door of the makeshift pub and walked in. Duncan and he were pretty full.

'How are you going to make the evening run?' asked Alex concerned for his friend. He knew the Captain wouldn't be going anywhere.

'I'm off again for the next four days as of this afternoon', informed Duncan. 'We're celebrating', he said, pouring out a quintuple measure for the friend that had just joined them.

'I'm celebrating too', said Alex. 'That's the last exam done. Five years of studying. Never again'. With that thought in mind he downed in one go the drink his friend handed to him.

'Slainte mhath ya bastard!' said the Captain again.

Alex tried to speak to Duncan discreetly, but in such a small confined space it wasn't easy. Mind you looking at the state of the Captain, he wasn't too sure he was taking it in, or at least the speech part of things.

'Aye, he's celebrating too', informed Duncan. 'He got a call an hour ago to say that after an investigation, the allegations against him had been found not to have been substantiated. Is that not right Captain?' he asked slapping him on his back.

'Slainte mhath ya bastard!' said the Captain yet again.

'So, I'm off for the weekend, you've finished your degree...'

'Diploma', interrupted Alex.

'Diploma, degree, doxology whatever. It's all the same to me', said Duncan heartily.
'And the Captain is an innocent man', he concluded turning to fill Alex's glass.

'Okay, maybe just one more', agreed Alex and he took the rather full glass from his friend. He avoided saying cheers to the Captain as he suspected he knew already what response he might get, but he felt satisfaction at the outcome of his plight.

'Aye, supposedly someone provided excrementary evidence on his behalf', Duncan went on to explain in his low highland droll.

'What evidence?' cried Alex.

'Aye, someone came forward to make a statement that was *ex-cre-mentary*', restated Duncan, trying to be so precise in his explanation and in his use of the word, which only made it all the more hilarious.

Alex laughed so hard his sides nearly burst.

'That's shite man. I think you mean…I think you mean', he tried to explain but couldn't get the words out for repressed laughter.

'What?' cried Duncan laughing at his friend's uncontrollable laughter, and then the Captain joined in too.

'It's not…it's not excrementory', cried Alex. 'That's…that's shite man!'

'It's not shite!' protested Duncan. 'It's bloody true'.

'Excrement is shite man', said Alex trying to compose himself as best as he could to get a full explanation out. 'I think the word you are looking for is *exculpatory*', but by this time he was lying on the floor and even Duncan saw the error and joined him.

Back at the Croft house Christina MacLean was looking at the clock wondering what was going on. She understood that Alex had needed to console himself and appease the feelings of guilt that he was carrying on the day of Fiona's funeral, but it was most unlike him not to be there at five o'clock for dinner.

'Oh, I think you'll find he's at Duncan's', her younger son informed her when she expressed her exasperation verbally. Just then Alex walked through the door.

'Sorry I'm late. I went to see Duncan for a few drinks to celebrate finishing my exams and my course', he explained.

'Of course dear', she said. 'Well done, that must be such a relief for you'.

'Yes, well done lad', agreed his father.

It was only later that night when she was lying in bed that she wondered how Malcolm knew where his brother had gone. She comforted herself with the thought that maybe it was a good sign, and they were on speaking terms again.

REVELATION

John MacLean woke feeling a dull pain in his head and was overcome by nausea.

He rose quietly so as not to disturb his wife and went through the sitting room. He was careful not to cause the floorboard to creak in the narrow corridor that passed Malcolm's room.

As he entered the clock on the mantlepiece struck six, which meant it was five in the morning. He made himself a cup of tea and sat on the chair and thought about things.

Then he went over to the sideboard and took out a box that was inlaid with brass strips down each side of the lid.

He took out some papers and took a pen from the table at the side of his chair and started to write instructions about bank accounts, paying council tax and the bin days on them. Taking out the brown envelope that contained his recently amended will, he sat back and read it drinking his tea which was by now lukewarm. He reached into the bottom of the box where he found his stash of dark chocolate. Although he was beginning to warm to his strict diet, he still needed some luxuries in life, he thought.

As he sat there savouring the rich taste, John wondered if the croft would continue to be handed down to the next generation, as it had been by his forebears until it was his name that held the tenancy. He had no concerns that Malcolm would look after it, and also ensure that Christina had a home for life, but he wondered if there would be a future generation of crofters after that.

Young people nowadays, with the exception of Malcolm and a few others left on the island, had little interest in maintaining a way of life that was becoming increasingly hard to produce any sort of sustainable income from. Occasionally people would come to the island, and similarly on Skye too, with wealth they had accumulated down south and had set out to live 'the good life' as they termed it. Often, they would either buy up some land and try and live a crofting lifestyle as they saw it, but after finding it generated little income and was not always a pleasant affair in the dark winters' mornings in the middle of a gale, they would sell up and return to the mainland. Occasionally someone would obtain a crofting tenancy, only to deregister some of the crofting land at a later date, reducing the prospects for others. The increasing demand for fewer crofting tenancies made the crofting life precarious. The Government had committed to increase the number of crofting tenancies, but such developments were few and far between.

He sat there lamenting for times past and realised he was getting older as he did not like all the changes that he saw round about him. He thought about his son Alex, and how he epitomized the younger generation. They had no desire to stay on the island, nor had they the slightest interest in their heritage or history for that matter.

As for Gaelic, few if any of the islanders spoke to one another in the native tongue anymore. It was a language which people used as catchphrases to enrich the conversation.

Despite his prophecy of doom, he had to acknowledge the Gaelic College on Skye and the new Distillery on Raasay were definitely positive developments. They had also managed, after a long fight, in which the N.H.S. in Inverness ignored their needs and were wholly culpable, to secure the new nurses on the island. The shop had changed hands and was now owned as a community asset too. But the island would never again hold the number of families which it once had, before the Clearances.

He rose and put the box back in the sideboard, being careful to leave his will, the bank details and some household instructions clearly on the top of the contents, so that they would be visible on opening it. He no longer felt nauseous and went back to lie down in bed, satisfied with what he had achieved in this early part of the morning.

Malcolm awoke to what he thought was the creak of the floorboards, but reasoned he must have imagined it. He noted however once he had had a bath, that the kettle was warm, so he suspected someone must have been up.

He knew it was Janice's day at the surgery so he knew he must check with his father if he needed any medication from it, or to make a request on his behalf for a repeat prescription. It had become increasingly hard for Janice and him to see one another regularly or more than momentarily because of the lockdown, though there were indications that it would be loosened. England had already decided to re-open shops and allow people to meet outdoors from different households.

Malcolm decided to go and collect what eggs there were and bring them in for his mother to use for breakfast. When he returned to the house Christina MacLean was indeed fluttering about and was glad to receive them for the poached egg on toast she was about to make for her husband.

'I can just hear him when I go through with this', she laughed to her son mimicking her husband's voice, *'Have we not got any fried eggs?'*

Malcolm laughed because he knew that was exactly what he'd say. Then he remembered, 'Oh Mum, do you need me to pick up anything from the surgery with it being Wednesday?'

'Yes dear, in fact I do. Could you call in and ask them for your Dad's new prescription. Is Janice working at the surgery this morning?' she added with a glint in her eye.

'Aye, right enough Mum', he said, making out that he had not realised.

'Gosh, that's a coincidence', said Christina smiling as she left the sitting room with a tray in hand.

Malcolm listened at the lounge door.

'Now here you are dear, sit up and have this before you get up', he heard his mother say.

'Oh, thank you dear', his father replied, and just as Malcolm was about to pull his ear away from the lounge door, he heard him ask, 'Have we not got any fried eggs?'

He laughed.

Alex was out on the porch of his Pod doing his yogic impression. He too wondered when the lockdown would end. He knew he had not been strict in adhering to it, though fortunately there were no known cases of the virus having reached Raasay, yet.

He was clear about what he would be doing today, but less so about what the future might bring, or for that matter, what he wanted from it. He even found himself momentarily envisaging what an island life would look like for him, but then he emerged from his trance, arriving back at his reality of feeling dissatisfied with such a lifestyle. It is so quiet, he thought, and everyone knows everything about what is going on. That's why he was so surprised that no-one had noticed the missing whisky, or had observed their operation to remove it from the distillery.
He laughed aloud.

Despite his feelings of restlessness, which it has to be said had lessened over the last month, he was looking forward to doing the tasks he had set out to do that day.
So, he got dressed and after a quick tidy of the Pod, he set off for Jean MacKay's house.

Now as fate would have it, Malcolm was under strict instructions from his father to go to the stores without his mother's knowledge and get some dark chocolate for him.

As his mother said to him with a grin as he was leaving the house, 'mind don't forget that prescription dear when you are getting your Dad's paper', she then muttered the word 'chocolate' to him before adding, 'and will you see if they have any flour in yet?'

When he reached the shop, Malcolm collected the Press and Journal and the not so secret dark chocolate bar and sat in the car reading the headlines. Having found little else other than news about the pandemic, which he had probably already caught up with that morning on the television, he set off for the surgery.

'You just missed Janice', the receptionist said to him when he got there.

'Oh', he said, feeling dejected.

'Yes, she had to go out and attend to a patient', she said.
This shook him a little but then she added, 'you brother also collected your Dad's prescription too when he was here. You're not having a lot of luck today Malcolm'.

She smiled to console him over his misfortunate timing.

'My brother was here?' he asked surprised.

'Yes', replied the receptionist, 'he went with her too'.

'What?' asked Malcolm, unsure that he had understood her correctly.

'Yes, she took your brother with her', she informed him.

He was frozen to the spot.

When Malcolm, feeling dazed, climbed back into the car, he thought about it more and more, before turning the key in the ignition and driving off at speed.

When he reached the croft house he dumped the newspaper and the chocolate rolled up in it at the side of his father's chair, before returning outdoors. From the driveway he just happened to catch Janice's car heading back down the road towards Inverarish, and he marched up the driveway and onto the road.

As he strode up the road, he reached the house of the old lady Jean MacKay, whom he had helped set her fire each day during the winter months until she was feeling a bit stronger.
He wasn't too surprised to see Alex coming out the door, as he thought that she was one of Janice's patients, and when he had seen her car go by, he just knew that was where she must have been.

Alex however was surprised to see his brother, and was taken aback when he reached the bottom of the steps that led up to the old woman's house to find that his brother had pushed his shoulder and had shouted something about him not being able to wait for the opportunity.

'Opportunity for *what exactly*?' he had retorted equally as abruptly.

'For trying to get in with Janice behind my back. I'm not stupid!' his brother hollered at him.

Alex couldn't recall seeing him so angry before. He was angry the day they had had the fight in the potato field, but there was almost a hatred oozing from his face.

'Now wait a minute before you get...', he tried to explain, but it was too late. His brother had hit him hard on the jaw, so much so that he recoiled backwards. Alex braced himself and the two brothers started struggling before falling to the ground.

'Stop it, you're a mad man!' cried Alex. As he lay there being completely overpowered by his brother, he retaliated and spat in his face, telling him 'she was gagging for it mate'.

Enraged, Malcolm struck him with a clenched fist across his cheek. Indeed, he was about to do it again, when he heard the voice behind him.

'Malcolm MacLean, don't you dare!' the old woman shouted at him with a look of shock on her face.

He looked backwards enabling his brother to wrestle himself free and escape from his clutches.

'You should be utterly ashamed of yourself', she added appearing to be almost overcome with anger herself.

Alex left the scene and headed in the direction of the potato field. Meanwhile Malcolm looking sheepish, but having always been respectful of his elders, issued an apology to Jean who just stood there shaking her head.

'Whatever did you do that for laddie?' she asked in disbelief.

'It doesn't matter Mrs. MacKay', he said. 'I am sorry to have brought it to your door'.

'It looks as if it matters very much indeed' she said. 'It's not the door that you need to apologise to, but your brother', she added emphatically.

Malcolm was indignant.

'I won't apologise to *that*', he said with revulsion in his voice.

'I think you should come in here and talk about it Malcolm', she suggested, gesturing with her hand for him to come indoors. She sat him in the lounge, where he sat forward in the armchair. She then went and brought him some tea.

'What is eating away at you son?' she asked. 'Whatever your brother has done, it cannot be so bad surely that you have to go about knocking lumps out of each other?'

'I'm…I'm not so sure Mrs. MacKay', he responded.

'What are you not sure about?' she asked trying not to sound impatient.

'Everything was fine till he came back', he responded.

'And it's not now, why not?' she pursued.

'Well, there's the way he treated Fiona, and now…', he informed.

'And now?' she asked suspecting what the problem might in fact be.

'And now he's trying to take Janice', he said both angrily but in a resigned manner.

'Nonsense laddie!' she exclaimed. 'Whatever is giving you that idea?'

'Well, she went with him this morning in the car when she never takes anyone in the car with her due to social distancing rules, and…', he rambled, but was stopped short.

'He was in the car Malcolm, but they were coming to see me', she laughed.

'I don't see what's so funny', he protested.

'Your brother, Alex, had called on me earlier this morning to see what I might like from the shops', she began.

'Alex?' he said in disbelief.

'Yes, your brother', she said. 'He's been getting my groceries for me at the stores for the last month'.

'Oh', said Malcolm surprised by the revelation, before adding, 'well it still doesn't explain why he and Janice were in the car together'.

'Yes, it does', the old woman explained. 'Alex could not get in or rouse me, or so he thought, and was worried something had happened to me. But I had simply forgotten to put my hearing aids in and I was round the back getting peat in'.

'So', she continued, 'he went to the surgery and the Doctor thought it was a good idea if Janice came up to check on me, so she brought your brother with her in case they needed to force entry'.

'Oh', said Malcolm still caught up in his thoughts.

'But what about, what about his trips to the surgery each Wednesday to see Janice?' he asked.

'Well, I don't know about him seeing Janice, as you say Malcolm, but he called into the surgery every Wednesday morning when it was open, for me, to collect my prescriptions that are made up each week in special dosage boxes, and then he'd pick up my groceries from James in the shop and bring them up here to me. It really was very kind of him'.

'Oh shit', said Malcolm holding his head in his hands.

When he eventually returned to the croft house and made his revelation, which both his parents were already very aware of, he was fully accepting of their displeasure and felt very humbled.

But just as equally displeased was his girlfriend Janice, who found that in just a matter of months, she was standing there again applying dressings to his elder brother's face.

When she thought about it more later that afternoon, she started to wonder if Malcolm just couldn't control his temper and was a bit too much of a risk to be around.

ON-CALL

Once again Janice found that this was another Wednesday that just seemed to be busier than ever. So, it was no surprise when she received a call from the G.P. who had just returned to the mainland to ask her to attend to the croft house at Oscaig.

For a moment she had wondered if things had escalated further when she asked her to attend that address, but she was quick to explain to her that Christina MacLean had phoned because her husband, John, appeared to have had another episode again.

'I'm not too happy', said the G.P. 'This appears to be the second episode that we know about, in as many months', she said. 'Err on the side of caution Janice, if you feel his physical functioning is impaired in any way, I think you just have to phone the ambulance and maybe contact the ferry office. There's a boat at half five, but even if you can't make that one in time, don't worry, just phone them and they'll make some arrangement with you'.

As Janice drove the couple of miles to the house, she was not surprised to be greeted by an anxious Malcolm in the driveway. She wanted to say something about his aggressive behavior, but knew this was neither the time or the place.

'He's in the lounge', said Malcom anxiously showing her in through the croft house door which she cleared without having to duck.

She found John in the armchair, and his wife Christina, by his side.

'You again', she joked to him.

'You came to take away my chocolate', he quipped, which she knew was a good sign.

However, having taken his pulse and his blood pressure, and having got him to try and hold his arm up, she was fairly certain he had lost some power in the one side.

She took Christina into the kitchen area of the room and whispered that she was going to have to transfer him to Portree. Christina understood, but knew she would not be able to go with him because of restrictions in attending the hospital on account of the coronavirus.

'I'm going to have to get you over to Portree John', Janice told him.
'Can I use your phone?' she asked them.

'Yes, certainly my dear', said Christina.

'If you could pack a small case or something for him', she suggested as she picked up the receiver.

When she came off the phone, she asked Malcolm if he would help get his father out to her car.

'I'll come with you if you want', he offered, to which she agreed.

Once Christina had filled a small case, she took it to the car while Malcolm walked with his father out to the car and put him in the passenger seat. Janice then let Malcolm into the rear seat, and before long they were driving down to the pier by the Big House. It was just after five thirty and the ferry had waited for them both. They were greeted by two paramedics who took John MacLean onto the boat. Malcolm stood and watched as the small craft rounded the pier head on its way to Sconser.

'It's best he gets checked out', Janice consoled him.

'It's happening too regularly now', he replied.

'All the more reason we need to get it checked out now', she reiterated. 'A lift home?' she offered.

'Please', he said.

As they drove back up the road from which they had come, Janice decided she needed to broach the subject.

'I heard what happened today', she said slightly more harshly than she had intended.
She tried to soften it. 'You know Malcolm, I know you and your brother have issues, but punching someone in the head is not a good way to resolve matters'.

'I know, but...', he tried to say.

'There's really *no* excuses for that sort of behaviour', she said as the car drew to a halt on the driveway. 'I really don't know if I want a boyfriend that can't keep his fists to himself'.

'But I thought…'

'I don't care Malcolm, it is not a good look', she added, leaning over towards him. He had thought she might be leaning over to kiss him, but instead the door was opened wide. No affection was shared and he got out the car. She drove off.

When he got in the house, his mother was just standing there as if she was disorientated. She then sparked into life.

'We need to let Alex know', she said.

Malcolm looked around as his brother was the last person in the world that he really wanted to have anything to do with. He had probably lost his girlfriend because of him.

'Will you go down the field and tell him?' his mother asked.

What else can I do? he thought, and he walked out the door and headed towards the potato field.

As Janice sat down to dinner that night, she wondered if she had done the right thing.

A man who can't keep his fists to himself was not something she was willing to countenance. She had seen her own mother suffer from it, and she was not going to see history repeat itself.

THE BRIEF VISITATION

Alex saw his brother approach the Pod door and was quick onto his feet. He was not going to be caught unawares by him again, and he was still nursing a sore jaw from the first encounter earlier in the day.

He opened the pod door.

'What do you want?' he asked as his brother approached, but received no answer.

'I'm not going to fight you Malcolm', he said firmly.

'I've not come to fight', said Malcolm in sombre tones which his brother noted.

For a moment he thought Malcolm had come to apologise, but when he heard the news all thoughts of it escaped from his mind.

It was such a frustrating thing.

As there was no G.P. on the island, their father had to go to the hospital on the ferry.

They could not visit, not even a brief visitation was allowed due to the restrictions caused by the pandemic. That would be hard on mother, he had said to his brother who readily agreed with him. All they could do was keep in touch using the phone and get updates from the hospital that way.

As Alex lay in bed that night looking out at the stars through the window of the Pod, he wondered if this would all mean he was going to be expected to take on the croft in his name. This was not a lifestyle he wanted, not now, not ever.

Malcolm too lay in bed that night wondering what more he could do to help both his mother and father at this time. He felt helpless. He also felt that he was responsible for the stress that was caused and that it was perhaps the reason his father had suffered possibly another 'mini-stroke' as Janice had termed it.

He was angry with himself too for showing Janice that he could not walk away as she had told him to do on the previous occasion.

Christina MacLean was up early the next morning and had already phoned the hospital by the time her son Malcolm came through.

The staff nurse on duty had been very helpful, and had even let her speak to her husband. She also had reassured Christina to call at any time if she found herself worrying during the night, as there are always people here even overnight, she had been told.

John had had a comfortable night and the Doctors wanted to run some tests over the next few days, she had been told. As they would want the results before deciding what to do next while observing him, she was not to expect his return this week.

Malcolm checked with his mother if she needed anything from the village and made her a cup of tea. They sat down together at the breakfast table.

'You know it grieves me', she said.

'I know Mum', he said, 'when I think about it, I cannot remember too many occasions you and Dad have not been together'.

'That's true Malcolm, but that's not what I was talking about', she informed him.

'Oh', Malcolm replied.

'I'm just so sad the pair of you can't seem to get along with one another anymore', she said.

There was a long silence before she added more to her opening.

'Your brother is not very good at showing his true feelings, whereas you do Malcolm. There are things he is good at, and you have things he'll never be any good at, but you need to let that be and accept it for what it is'.

'I know Mum', said Malcolm.

'I always remember how my brother, your Uncle Alex, seemed to get all the opportunities', she told him. 'And yet I always seemed to get better marks than he did at his school subjects, but it was always Alex my parents idolized and pushed forward'.

'He was a lawyer?' her son queried.

'Yes, he was a good lawyer too. My Dad and Mum, your Gran and Grampa MacLeod, always used to push him forward and I was viewed as being no more than a future housewife. And I was so so jealous of him', she protested with a little bit of resentment sounding in her voice. He had never heard her speak like that before.

'But then I accepted Malcolm, that he wasn't to blame for that. It was just the way people were brought up in my day'.

'But that's not fair Mum', Malcolm protested by proxy.

'No, it wasn't fair Malcolm, but it wasn't his fault. It was the way society was at that time. So, what I am saying is I realised there was no point feeling bitter about things, it's just the way they are and is the deck life deals you sometimes'.

'I think I see what you're saying Mum', he replied.

It was sometime later that day when he was in the village collecting groceries for his mother, that he thought more about it.

'Not seen your brother today', said James. 'Do you know if he's going up to old Stuart's today?' he asked.

'Old Stuart, what Stuart Kennedy?' he asked. 'Why would he be going up there?'
He sounded confused.

'Aye, Stuart Kennedy', said the shopkeeper, 'I sometimes wonder if you two speak to each other'.
He said it before he realised it was out of his mouth, as he had heard about the fracas outside Jean MacKay's house, as had the whole island by now.
'I didn't mean it like that', he said.

'No, no, fair's fair', said Malcolm acknowledging he had been the talk of the island.

'He's been helping cut his peat and some for Jean MacKay over the last three or four weeks', informed James.

As he walked out the door of the stores, his heart leapt as he saw Janice. He waved enthusiastically but she just waved back and walked on towards the nurses' house without stopping. He was deeply saddened.

He liked the sound of the waves and decided to take his deep thoughts down to the pier. As he stood below the two mermaid statues that bankrupted a Clan Chief, he lamented the fact that he had blown it with Janice. She was so beautiful, he thought, her legs were like silk and her blue eyes radiated the kindness that was in her heart, which was so evident when she had been dealing with his father. He was conscious that he was almost feeling tearful, when a voice interrupted.

'How you doing Malkie?' shouted big Duncan Nicolson who was the deckhand on the ferry. He was also his brother's closest friend on the island.

'Aye, no bad', said Malcolm not sounding very convincing.

'Sorry to hear about your Pa,' said Duncan. 'I saw him when he came on the ferry yesterday. Hopefully he'll be back with you soon'.

'Hope so', said Malcolm.

'Here', said Duncan noticing his dejected manner, 'the number of people I see being taken over to the Hospital on the ferry you would be shocked at', he said. 'And most of them come back too', he added.

Malcolm managed to muster his first smile in twenty-four hours, more because of Duncan's rather poor attempt to be comforting than by any words of consolation that he in fact had offered.

'Did you hear what your brother did?' he asked Malcolm.

'No', said Malcolm, and as he walked up the road with Duncan, the latter recounted to him the tale of the Captain's suspension and how it turned out his brother who had helped them when the incident had happened, had contacted the ferry company to put them right on the facts.

'He didn't have to do that', he told Malcolm.

'No, I guess he didn't', said Malcolm.

As he walked up the road towards the croft house, he was in such deep thought that he forgot that he had taken the car. He was seriously having to re-evaluate his tainted view of his brother. A brother who he had thought was trying to wrestle his girlfriend from him, had summoned help for Jeannie MacKay believing her to have had an accident; had taken groceries and medication to her each week; had helped Stuart Kennedy dig his peats, and had advocated on behalf of the Captain of the ferry.

THE RETURN LEG

In relation to his brother, Malcolm was caught up in his thoughts and was beginning to go through a process of re-evaluating his view of him. Meanwhile his brother was feeling increasingly scared. Scared that his father was going to die, scared that he would have to organise the funeral, and scared that he'd be expected to take on the croft.

His sense of angst was increased sharply the next day when, before he called for dinner at five o'clock at the croft house, he found the Episcopalian Minister visiting. For a moment he wondered if his father had died.

Dinner was a largely subdued affair, with Alex wrapped up in his thoughts of gloom and doom, and Mrs. MacLean wondering with the weekend approaching whether or not her husband would get home next week. The one positive of it all she noted, was that Malcolm was trying to be civil to his brother again. Her husband's illness was in a strange sort of way maybe bringing them together again, she thought.

Her momentary elation however was brought to an end when on Monday there was still no prospect of her husband making the return leg of his journey to the hospital.

It was a return trip too that found Janice visiting Jean MacKay for a new round of treatment. The ulcer on her leg had returned and she was being asked to attend to it again each day. She enjoyed the conversation with the older woman, and viewed her like she viewed her own Gran.

'I am sick of it', she said. 'It's fine for a few months, then pow, it's back again'.

'Oh, we'll soon get on top of it', reassured Janice in her enthusiastic way.

'And how's the romance?' she asked the young nurse, not reserved in coming forward.

'Dead', she said emphatically.

'Oh, why's that dear?' she asked.

'I think that would be obvious', she said, before adding, 'after what happened here'.

'It's not that obvious my dear', she said in a kindly voice, 'try me'.

'Well, you know, Malcolm knocking lumps out of his brother. I really don't like someone who can't control his temper and resorts to violence like that'.

'I understand', said the older woman. 'I used to have a husband like that', she informed, which made the nurse look up at her in surprise.
'Oh yes, in these days we just had to grin and bear it, but an absolute *bastard* he was!'

Janice laughed not meaning to, but she was just so taken aback at Jean MacKay's expression. She laughed too.

'A dog's life he gave me. I can never forgive him for that' she said, with much more seriousness in her voice.

'That must have been awful', said Janice and then she shared some of her own personal history.

'Having heard what you say, I am not surprised you are wary of a man who is quick to anger', said the older woman, 'but can I say this to you?'

'Yes, go on', said Janice not sure what she was going to say to her.

'Malcolm MacLean is not like that', she said.

'But he thumped his brother', Janice protested.

'He did it is true, but between you and me he probably had it coming for at least eighteen years. Did you know why he hit him?' she asked.

'It makes no difference', said Janice emphatically.

'Sure, but he thought Alex had been trying to win your affection behind his back, but I also think he thought he was defending your honour'.

'How?' asked the young nurse.

'Well', said the old woman, 'and I'm sorry to say it, because he has been ever so helpful to me over the last three or four weeks too, but Alex MacLean has a bit of a track record'. Then she looked thoughtful before explaining further. 'Let's just say when it comes to women, yourself included I'm afraid, he needs to wash his mouth out with soap and water'.

'Oh' said Janice.

'I think your Malcolm is in my opinion dear, probably the gentlest boy I have known. I have never known him to lift a hand to anyone in all the years I have known him and that's why I was so shocked'.

'Oh' said Janice again, less sure of herself. 'Well, he's not *my* Malcolm MacLean anymore', she added defensively.

'Well, that's a shame', came the response. 'Can I tell you a little secret?' asked the older woman.

'Go on', said Janice unsure as to what was going to come next.

'When I heard the commotion I went outside, and I stood there shocked, because I saw that Malcolm was about to hit his older brother, which he did. And when he did, I thought shall I stop it? But having heard what Alex had said to him about you, I didn't. Instead, I found inside I was egging him on, hoping he'd give him a right belter, and then I thought I better say something when he did exactly that'.

She laughed, and Janice too found her first opportunity to smile about the doomed relationship since the events of that day.

As she drove down the road and back towards the village, she was in two minds whether or not to call in and see how Christina MacLean was managing, but she decided against it as she still felt she did not want to be embroiled in the family tensions.

Dinner on the Tuesday night was an equally subdued affair.

Christina was still getting told that her husband was in for observation. They had exchanged a few words on the phone, but it was impossible to tell in that short call whether or not he was any better.
The hospital staff told her what they could, but she really wanted to know if he was going to be coming home soon and they just could not tell her this information.

Christina had gone to do some ironing in the bedroom after doing the dishes with Malcolm. Alex just sat at the table and thought about how this was all going to end.

'I hope they don't expect me to take on the croft', said Alex.

'I don't think anyone is thinking like that just now', Malcolm replied.

Alex got up and headed out the door. He was going to return to the potato field, but then decided to go down the road and see Duncan. As so often happened when the two got together, it ended up as a night in the makeshift pub.
Nearly three months had passed since they raided the distillery and the water butt was beginning to drain slowly.

'I reckon there is maybe only about ten or twenty bottles worth left in there', said Duncan.

It did not stop them draining the tank even further.

'You know I think my Da' is going to die', Alex informed his friend.

'What makes you say that?' asked his friend.

'I don't know. Bad things come in threes as they say', he proposed.

'And what are the three?' asked Duncan.

'Well, first there was Fiona dying, then there was the fight with Malcolm, and now my Da' is dying', he said.

'I saw Malcolm the other day', Duncan informed his friend. 'He didn't seem that angry at you. Why did he hit you anyway?' he asked.

'I think he thought I was after his woman?' he replied.

'And were you?' laughed his friend.

'No!' said Alex, 'but yes I would give her one if that is what you are asking me'.

'I'm not surprised he's suspicious of you', said his normally unreflective friend.

'I think when I told him she was gagging for it, it put him over the edge', said Alex.

'Well, no wonder he hit you mate', said Duncan.

'Aye, I suppose you're right. I wouldn't do that anyway to my own brother', he said, but even Duncan wasn't too sure about that one.

As Alex made the return trip to the potato field, he started to think of his father's fate once again.

NIGHT OF THE VERY LONG FACES

The next night was as equally a depressing night at the family dinner table. Christina had been promised a call by the Doctor to discuss her husband's progress or lack of it, but no call had been forthcoming. She had called the hospital at tea time only to be told the Doctor had now left, and that all that had been decided was to keep her husband in for further observation.

Alex was becoming increasingly anxious that his father was going to die, but did not want to verbalise it for fear of upsetting his mother.
Christina herself also harboured some deep-rooted fears which were exacerbated when she opened the wooden box in the sideboard to look for the bankcard, only to find a list of bank account details, her husbands amended will, and notes about what days to put the bins out and pay the council tax by.
Malcolm was sensitive to the feelings of everyone around him. In fact, he had an uncanny knack of feeling emotions other people were feeling, which was as much a burden as it was a bonus.

When he and Alex were alone, he knew his brother wanted to get something off his chest.

'You're restless', he simply observed.

'I was just thinking about all the grief I gave Dad about the croft and island life and not wanting to be here anymore', he said.

'You had all your exams to come. It was a stressful time for you', Malcolm suggested.

'And you're right if it makes you feel better. I wasn't nice to Fiona'.

And then much to Malcolm's surprise his brother started to cry. He hadn't seen him cry since, well Primary School maybe, so he felt a bit helpless to respond.

'I made a mess of it, Malcolm, and caused them unhappiness', he sobbed. 'Look, I even lied to you about your girl'.

'I know, I know', said his younger brother. 'But you know what Alex? We all make mistakes. Look at me and Janice. I fucked that one up. But we all get a second chance in life, maybe just not always at the things we want', he said remorsefully before adding, 'but it's never too late'.

'I know', said his brother, 'but I wouldn't know where to start'. He sniffled and cried contracting his body in towards himself.

'But you have Alex, you have. Look at what you did for Jeannie the other day and the other weeks too, for Stuart Kennedy, for the Captain. That is taking action to do something positive, it's not just thinking about it which we are all too good at doing sometimes'.

Christina MacLean had returned from her room which she was tidying, as she tried to keep herself busy to keep her mind off things. When she returned to the lounge, she momentarily noticed that her two boys were sitting close to one another, and it was then that someone knocked at the door.

'I'm not expecting anyone', she said heading towards it, and she looked at her sons.

'No, me neither', said Alex trying to regain his composure.

'No', said Malcolm who was also surprised by the late caller.

When she opened the door, it was Janice the young nurse.

'I hope you don't mind me calling', she said. 'I was up visiting a patient and the Doctor asked me to call in and give you a message'.

Alex looked at his brother alarmed. Christina also looked concerned given the time of night.

'You better come in', invited Christina and Janice came in and sat on the edge of one of the dining room seats.

'The Doctor apologises as she got called away, so she never got to speak with you Mrs. MacLean', said Janice. 'She just wanted to let you know they have adjusted John's medication and he is ready to come home on Friday. The ambulance will bring him to the boat, but if one of you could meet him at the pier that would be great'.

'Oh, that's great news', said Christina unable to contain herself. She grabbed Janice's hand in delight to shake it warmly.

As he choked, Alex said, 'thank God, I thought he was going to die'.

'Alex!' cried his mother.

'Great!' exclaimed Malcolm.

'Anyway, I just thought I would call in and tell you the good news, rather than you having to wait until tomorrow to hear it'.

Janice rose to leave.

'Oh, thank you dear, thank you dear', said Christina MacLean again. As the young nurse opened the door to leave, Christina MacLean looked towards her son, Malcolm, but he did not move.

She followed her out the door.

'Thank you again so much my dear'.

'Goodbye Mrs. MacLean' she said and drove off picking up some gravel behind her wheel as she disengaged her clutch.

As she drove back to the village her mind drifted off the road, but fortunately she was soon back at the nurses' house.

Later that night when Alex was gone, Christina MacLean surprised her younger son.
'What is wrong with the men in my family?' she asked him.

'What do you mean Mum?' asked Malcolm unsure if she was referring to his father's health, or to something Alex and he had done.

'Why did you not go and speak to Janice before she left?' she asked. 'She noticed', she added.

'I don't think she wants to see me', he responded.

'Rubbish' said his mother, 'she wouldn't have called in otherwise'.

'But she came to tell us about Dad', he protested.

'I don't think so, she could have just as easily have phoned to tell me. Sometimes you know Malcolm', she said, 'it's only when someone is gone that we truly find out that we loved them. Don't be like your brother and let that happen to you too'.

With that parting thought, she went across to the phone and phoned one of her close friends.

Malcolm tried not to think on his misfortune as he lay there that night with a long face. Janice had been the first girlfriend he had really had and he knew in her eyes, her opinion of him was probably as low as you could get.

When he awoke the next morning, it was a stormy affair outside, and after deliberating on whether or not to move the chickens, which he decided against, he decided after breakfast to go into the village to collect the paper and to try again to get his mother some flour, which had become like gold dust during the pandemic.

'Oh, and will you get two bars of dark chocolate for your Dad coming back?' his mother had asked, which really was like gold dust to his father.

She was taking the car this morning to visit her friend, Rhona MacLeod, who lived in the north of the island. He didn't mind walking. It was certainly windy, but it was not raining.

Passing by the potato field he noticed how the light in his brother's glamping pod was on. He thought he would go down and ask if he wanted anything, but decided against it. He knew his brother liked to get out into the main village and would undoubtedly prefer to make the trip himself at some point during the day.

As he walked along the road it was in the back of his mind that the stormy weather might affect the ferry the next day. Usually there was a period of calm after the storm but certainly at the moment, it did not look like easing off any.

As he sat in the pod, Alex was having similar thoughts.
After his night of the long face at the dinner table, he had reflected much of the night on where the future lay for himself and had made some decisions. But first he needed to do something. He searched for his mobile phone which was always getting lost on the camp bed amongst the covers.

It was later in the morning when he was walking to Inverarish, a few hours after his brother's return trip, that Alex came across the small Ford Fiesta in the layby. Janice had stopped there. It had been the place where she and Malcolm used to meet on her way back from Jean MacKay's.
She opened the passenger door of the car and Alex climbed in.

A DEAD WEIGHT

It was Christina MacLean who said it first the next morning.

'I do hope your Dad gets back today with this storm', she said to her younger son at the breakfast table.

'Hope so', said her younger son. 'Oh', he said excited to tell her the news. 'James has some flour coming in this morning, so he said he would put it aside if I collected it this morning'.

'Do you know how much he'll stick by for us?' she asked, as she had doubted if the paper sack in the corner of the kitchen area could provide them with much more over the weekend.

'I asked him for two sacks, making thirty-two kilogrammes I think', he replied.

'You are my wee star', she grabbed his cheek in a sickly-sweet sort of way.

'Mum!' he grimaced.

'You'll need to take the car in for it', she suggested.

'Yes, it'll be in off the second boat, so I'll pick it up around mid-day'.

When Malcolm drove into the village he saw there was some debris on the road to Inverarish, caused by the gale. He stopped and removed it, got back in the car and drove along the high road to the community stores.

'Did it come?' he asked James.

'Aye', said the shopkeeper. 'Take your car up the back door and I'll stick it in for you'.

Malcolm was careful to hold the boot of the car securely in his hand as it was still quite stormy, and he did not want to tell his father that his car had been damaged on his return. He was worried that the boat might not be sailing, and decided to check. If there was anyone who would know, big Duncan would, and he knew he would probably be finishing up at the pier at this time doing their checks.

When he reached the pier, he noted that they were tying up until the later afternoon run and were going through some checks. He decided to wait for Duncan in the car. As he thought about the weight in the boot of the car, he smiled to himself to think there was no chance they would be blown away in the gale. He really hoped it would ease off, but if the ferry had made it in the morning, he could see no reason why it shouldn't make the afternoon and evening crossings.

Janice had been to see her patient, Jean MacKay, and was driving back down the road towards Inverarish. This was her last day as the on-call nurse and then she had the weekend off which she was pleased about, as it had been a really busy fortnight. She actually felt quite tired, and only had five hours to go before her colleague, Margaret, relieved her. When she reached the house, she put some beans in the microwave and started to toast the bread. She was determined to take the full hour she was entitled to as a lunch break, but had rarely succeeded in having this last fortnight.

It was the Captain who first noticed something was going on. Out the corner of his eye, he saw a woman running back and forward further along the pier, towards the quayside where the smaller crafts were moored.
He pointed to Duncan, but not having the advantageous viewpoint which the Captain enjoyed, he just shook his head as he was unsure what he was pointing at as he could see nothing.

In the water, unbeknown to either of them, a young boy had either fallen or somehow been swept into the water. His mother was frantic.

Malcolm had been walking round by the mermaids and had gone up the hill where the canon was, and could see in both directions.
He could see Duncan as he was high enough up to look straight ahead and onto the deck of the ferry, and he could also see the mother running around frantically crying for help on the quayside, which lay down the hillock on his right hand side.
He too pointed to Duncan before he made his way down the hill to help.

When he reached the woman who was hysterical by this time, all she could say to him was that her son had 'slipped on the seaweed and had been swept into the water'.

He looked and looked in the quay, but could not see anything. Seeing the lifebuoy in its casing at the other end of the quay, he was about to go over and get it but then he saw what he thought was the boy's head.

'Look', he said to her, pointing in the direction of the lifebuoy. 'Go and get the lifebuoy!'

She ran in the direction of the lifebuoy which was quite a distance away at the end of the old pier. There were some creels lying on the quayside, and Malcolm decided there was only one thing he could do. He threw off his shoes and started to descend the iron steps that led down to the where the small boats lay tied up. He didn't have time to loosen a boat and take it out, nor could he go all the way down the steps as the swell would make him hit the quayside wall if he tried to swim out from the point where it met the water. So, he jumped into the dark foamy water before he reached the bottom rung.

When he surfaced, he took a sharp intake of breath and struggled to inhale. His body was in shock as it was bitterly cold. He remembered from the lessons they had had at the Outdoor Centre, that he had to remain calm and try to breathe. The water crashed over his head. He began to swim to the shore side where he had seen the boy.

Meanwhile the Captain was now running along the quayside, and he reached the woman who had managed to release the lifebuoy from its casing and was beginning to run back to the shore side, which Malcolm was swimming towards.
Malcolm gulped the salty seawater, choking and spluttering. He was struggling hard to make much headway in the choppy water. After about only ten metres, he looked around frantically between the waves. He saw nothing.

The Captain was by now nearing the heather bank on the shore side, with the boy's mother close behind. He looked at the water but saw nothing other than Malcolm's struggles.

In the distance the sound of a motor boat could be heard approaching the same direction.

As the toast popped up shaking the toaster, so did the door.

'Unbelieveable!' said Janice aloud.

She opened the front door to the terraced cottage.

'You have to come quick', said the breathless voice. 'There's been an accident'.

That certainly got the adrenaline rushing, but Janice had to remember to stay calm and gather as much information as she could to assess the situation accurately.
Looking longingly at her toast and beans, she walked over to the side unit and picked up her bag of utensils.

'Where is the accident?' she asked.

'At the pier, at the pier', came the panicked response. 'Someone has drowned'.

This was not a situation she was used to dealing with, but as she and the youth drove down to the pier and to where the car was parked, she rehearsed in her mind the need first to assess for danger, and then the principles of resuscitation. Hopefully they were not too late.

Indeed, they were not too late at all. Malcolm had managed to reach the boy who was flapping his arms about wildly. He secured him around the neck and tried to bring him to the shore. But between the sea condition and the panicked response of the boy, he struggled to get close to the shore. It was then that two things for the better, or for the worse happened, which seemed to turn events partially in his favour.

When Janice and the youth got closer, and coming down by the access from behind the mound of rock and heather and onto the grassy bank, they could see the Captain repeatedly launching the lifebuoy but bringing it up empty each time. The boy's mother was standing on the shore shouting her son's name and sobbing loudly. Janice had once attended a car accident, but never anything quite like this.

It is never wise to sail too close to the rocks, but on this occasion, Duncan drew the ship's rescue vessel close to Malcolm, approximately ten meters from the rocky shore. He carefully leaned over the side and pulled the boy up from the water with Malcolm's help from the sea below. The boy had become lifeless and was a deadweight. But Duncan could not keep the boat stable enough to get his friend's brother, Malcolm, aboard too.

'Go! Go!' shouted Malcolm and Duncan looked back as he let the craft drive up to the seaweed bank, and from there the lifeless boy was raised by him and lifted on to shore by the Captain. The boy's mother was crying even louder seeing the state of her son. The Captain brought him over to the mound of grass in the shelter of the rock and laid him on the ground. Janice knelt over him. The youth who had taken her there, was also now crying loudly.

Meanwhile Duncan was looking back anxiously to see if he could spot Malcolm amongst the waves, and sighed a massive sigh of relief when he saw him dragging himself up on some ropes that were draped over the rocks and the seaweed. Malcolm reached a knoll of grass and lay on his back exhausted and tried to regain his breath.

Duncan took his small craft to the iron steps and quayside, tied it to a bollard, and made his way on foot to where the Captain, the mother and youth, and the nurse were all kneeling around the boy.
Janice was in the process of giving him mouth to mouth resuscitation during which he was sick and vomited over her uniform.

I forgot about that bit, she thought to herself, tears welling up in her own eyes that she had successfully brought him round. As she and the Captain rolled him into the recovery position, she looked up as if giving thanks and praise to a deity.
As the boy regained full consciousness and awareness of his surroundings, his mother nestled his head in her lap.

'So, who's the hero!' exclaimed Janice, turning round to look at Duncan.

'I'm no hero', he said which made her think for a moment that he was being very modest, then she saw a tearful and very wet Malcolm standing beside him. He was overcome by the emotion of it all relishing the fact that the boy had lived.

'Malcolm!' she cried.

THE RETURN OF THE KING

The boat did make the later crossings that day. One boy left Raasay on it for the hospital with his mother and brother to get checked out, and was met by the paramedics who did an exchange at Sconser, having brought with them another patient to the ferry, who had been discharged home.
The crossings were much gentler too, the sea state being much more subdued than it had been over the last few days.

Malcolm's earlier escapades were needless to say the gossip of the island, and his father had heard all about the events of the early afternoon from Duncan, who had gone over them in finite detail with a blow by blow account.

As he came off the boat he was met by his wife and elder son, Alex. Malcolm had been unable to drive home as his clothes were ringing wet, so Alex had walked in to collect the car to take it home and return with his mother later in the day to collect his father from the ferry.

Malcolm had been mildly hypothermic, so Janice took him to the nurses' cottage where she dried his clothes in the tumble drier as best as she could, sat him in a foil wrap to get his body heat stabilized, and then much to his embarrassment, particularly when the older nurse Margaret walked in, had sat him down with some tea giving him her bathrobe to wear, which barely fitted him and a towel to help him maintain his dignity.
Even the older nurse raised her eyebrows for a moment until she heard what had happened.

As Janice had to write up the notes and communicate with the hospital in Portree, Margaret gave Malcolm a lift home, once his clothes had been dried and returned to him, along with the restoration of his modesty.

On the journey home he said little and the older nurse tried to engage him in conversation.

'It's been quite a week for you, between your father being in the hospital and now this', she said with empathy in her voice.

When she dropped him off at the croft house, he thanked her.

'I'm sure we'll be seeing more of you', Margaret replied, which struck him as an odd thing to say. He had met her only on the one occasion before today.

When he got in, he found his father sitting on his armchair.

'I'm away for a few weeks and I come back to find my son is a super hero', he joked.

'Hardly', said Malcolm modestly. All he felt was washed out by the day's events.

As the next twenty-four hours unfolded, he noticed that his father was maybe a little slower doing things, but he did not know if he was deliberately taking it easier, or if in fact the mini-stroke had caused him to slow down.

Needless to say, Christina ran about him like a mother hen, and Alex came over to see if there was anything he could do on the croft to help the next morning. Malcolm too adopted his father's early morning chores so that the patriarch was left with nothing to do.

This will never do, he thought to himself.
At dinner that evening he thought he had better raise it.

'You've all been really helpful over the last day', he said, 'but if you do everything for me it will only make matters worse for me. I need to be able to do things', he said. 'I do not want to be some helpless old man who wastes away doing nothing and has everything done for him'.

'You know we are all just trying to help', said Christina trying to placate him.

'I know, I know you all are. But the crofting life is me, it's who I am', he said.
'If you take that away from me it would be like me losing my identity', he explained.

Alex immediately understood and realised simultaneously that this was why he struggled with island life.

As they finished dinner there was a knock at the door.

'I'm not expecting anyone', said Christina jumping up and heading towards it. She looked at her sons.

'No, me neither', said Alex.

'No', said Malcolm feeling a touch of deja-vu, given a similar occurrence and response from all the previous night.

When his mother opened the door, the feeling of déjà vu was reinforced. It was Janice the young nurse, though on this occasion she was not wearing her nurse's uniform anymore.

'I hope you don't mind me calling', she said.

'Come in lass', shouted John MacLean and Christina held the door open for her.

She came into the sitting area of the lounge cum kitchen.

'Take a seat', said Christina.

'I hope you don't mind me calling round to see how my favourite patient was before I finish for the week off', she joked.

'Well', said John, 'I'm fine, though I've not got a chance to be anything else', he replied looking at his wife and two sons.

'Ah', said Janice. 'Better to start off slow'.

'When you get older my dear, you do *everything* more slowly', he laughed.

Not too sure what to make of that comment, Christina offered Janice a cup of tea.

'No thank you Mrs. MacLean', she said. 'I only popped round for a moment just to see how John was getting on'. She rose to leave.

'That's very thoughtful of you my dear', said Christina MacLean, and as Janice went to leave, Malcolm was conscious that his mother was staring at him intently.

As Janice exited the croft house door, one of the few who didn't have to duck to leave safely by it, Christina MacLean was about to say to her son to follow her out.
But on this occasion, she did not have to.

A good half an hour later Malcolm returned indoors. His mother looked inquisitively, but his son gave nothing away. When she went to bed that night, she was glad to have her husband back with her by her side.

MEALTIME INTERRUPTIONS

The following day John was pleased to note that his younger son had left him his morning chores to do.

Christina too was pleased to note her husband was acting like his former self.

The only down side, which was a minor aberration on his day, was that Malcolm, uncharacteristically it has to be said, had forgotten to collect the daily newspaper.

'He's got an appointment', Alex informed him, but I will pick it up for you later.

'An appointment?' said his father. 'What kind of appointment?' he asked.

'I don't know Dad', Alex retorted. 'I'm not my brother's keeper, am I?'

'That's a biblical quote', chirped his father. Alex let it pass and deliberately avoided another science versus religion debate which he and his father had engaged in endlessly for many years now. It always ended the same way.

'Do you know what Malcolm's appointment is for today?' said John raising his voice so his wife could hear him.

'No idea', his wife called back over the noise of the mixer.

It was a beautiful day outside and the lockdown was easing, enabling people to mix with another household.

'I hope he's remembering to socially distance', quipped his father.

Alex stayed around the croft house during the late morning and early afternoon, as he was waiting for a letter in the post about a job he was interested in. He did not say anything to his parents but deftly maneuvered the letter into his pocket from the bundle of mail which "Andrew the Post" left on the doormat for them under a stone, before knocking the door to let them know it was there.

'Well, I wonder what we have today', said his father and he started to open the envelopes.

Alex took a drive down to the community stores and picked up the Press and Journal, and a Herald newspaper for himself.
On this occasion it was he who spotted his brother turning down the road to the Park, but unlike his younger brother, he did not follow him though he did wonder what he was doing. He had an appointment, but the Doctor's surgery wasn't open, so what appointment could he possibly have? he thought to himself.
But despite his modified behavior over the last few months, he was still a bit full of himself, and was soon thinking again about the job description he had received that morning. So, he drove home.

Christina found it odd that there were no eggs in the boxes she left out in the morning for Malcolm to collect and fill, and when she went out she found he had not collected them. It was completely out of character, but nothing was said and she collected them himself. In fact, he had even forgotten to put the bins out up by the roadside and she had to ask Alex to do it for her when he returned to the croft house with the newspapers.

Once he had taken the bins up to the road end, Alex walked into the main village where he met Duncan coming off the additional afternoon ferry.

'Is there any left?' he asked his friend.

'What the good stuff?' asked Duncan.

'Aye, the good stuff', said Alex and the two men went up to the makeshift pub at the Old Post Office and shared a few.

'I'm thinking of applying for this job', he told his friend.

'But that's not really teaching', said his friend a little surprised.

'I know', said Alex, 'but I don't think teaching is what I am'.

'What do your parents say about it?' asked big Duncan.

'I'm old enough not to need my parents say so on anything', Alex retorted.

'Aye, I know that. I just thought they might have a view about it. That's all', said big Duncan.

After a few drinks, Alex conscious of the time gave his apologies and left. He did not want to be late for dinner and cause anyone at the house any undue anxiety. Nevertheless, the two men had the obligatory 'one for the road'.

As he walked back to Oscaig he was feeling the heat. It had probably been the hottest day of the year so far, and was particularly welcome as to some extent people had been feeling a bit more confined indoors than they normally would over the last few months.

When he got back to the croft house at five minutes to five, he sensed his mother's anxiety and thought she was fretting at his almost late arrival.

'It's not like your brother', she muttered to him quietly, as she did not want to transfer her anxiety to her husband.

Right enough, thought Alex, he doubted if Malcolm had ever been late for a mealtime, or come to think of it, anything in his life.

'He's probably just chilling out after yesterday mother', he said. 'It was one helluva day for him'.

At ten minutes past the hour she started to serve the dinner.

'It's not like Malcolm to be late', John MacLean announced.

'He had a rather eventful day yesterday Dad', said Alex, giving the same explanation that he had just given to his mother.

'We'll just start without him then', said his father before closing his eyes to say the grace.

'Some hae meat and canna eat
And some would eat that want it;
But we hae meat and we can eat
And sae the Lord be thankit'.

Not the most original, thought Alex to himself, but bit his tongue.

They did not have to worry about Malcolm however.
He was only fifteen minutes late, and came bursting through the door a bit breathless.

'Sorry I'm late, Mum, Dad', he said.

'It's okay', said his mother getting to her feet to retrieve a plated meal from the hot surface of the Aga cooking stove. Noticing he had left the door open, she asked him to 'remember to close the door'.

'No Mum', he said which took her aback, 'I've got something I want to tell you. To tell you both'.

'Go on lad', said his father.

At this point Janice walked in from behind the door.

'Mum, Dad, I want you to meet my new fiancée'.

'Oh, that's wonderful!' cried his mother, clasping her hands together in delight.

Before long the new member of the family was showing them the ring that Malcolm had got that morning from "The Silver Grasshopper", the only jewellery shop on the island.

'That's beautiful', said Christina MacLean to her future daughter-in-law, and a tear of joy welled up in her eye.

CEILIDH

It was not until the following August that the couple were finally wed, once the restrictions on indoor and outdoor gatherings had been lifted.

As well as the married couple, everyone was taken with the new island whisky that had just been released, and which no-one had tasted before. Alex, Duncan and needless to say the Captain were not quite so sure about that, but said nothing to anyone about it.
In fact, the only person who had not tasted the whisky by the end of the night was Ian, the night watchman at the distillery. Ironically, he did not drink alcohol, just too many sugary drinks instead.

The distillery shop had re-opened several months after lockdown, but a decision was made not to resume the tours around the distillery for the remainder of the season, so no-one was any wiser that one of the barrels which sat in the distillery was in fact empty.

'I didn't think you would want me as your best man', Alex confided in the bridegroom. 'Not after all that happened between us', he said.

'Of course, I wanted you to be my best man', said Malcolm. 'Who else could I possibly have chosen?'

'Well, there's…', but Alex was interrupted.

'No, I mean, who else is there I know?' laughed Malcolm.

'Cheeky', said his brother. There was a pause. 'You know I'm leaving in the New Year', Alex said.

'Oh', said Malcolm. 'Leaving to do what?' he asked a little surprised given the time of year he intended for his departure.

'I think I am going to go and work for a charity overseas teaching kids English', he informed him.

'I thought you were feeling happier here', Malcolm observed.

'I am, but I think it's time to leave the pig pod', he laughed.

The night was a very lively affair. As Alex watched his brother, he felt remorse that this had not been a celebration for Fiona and him, but realized that only he was to blame for that.

As the night wore on, he broke the news of his forthcoming departure to his mother and father.

The new Community Centre was the perfect setting for the ceilidh, allowing for Eightsome Reels and "Strip the Willow", among other Highland dances. Needless to say, Mrs. MacLeod of Raasay was played on the pipes and the whisky flowed.

Duncan found he had great difficulty telling everyone that it had been an *Episcopalian* wedding, and the Captain found he was able to use his familiar greeting to great effect, though who the bastards were no-one was quite sure.

Janice looked stunning in her wedding dress and just as stunned when her hair was showered with shortbread crumbs, when they reached the Community Centre for the reception. Her bridesmaid, Margaret, the older nursing colleague, who was delighted to have caught the bouquet, had explained it was an old Raasay tradition.
Janice was pretty sure crumbs were still appearing in the shower several weeks thereafter.

Before the couple departed for the night, Margaret turned to Malcolm and said to him,

'I told you so'.

'You told me so?' said Malcolm a little confused.

'I told you that night in the car that we'd be seeing more of you', she laughed.

With few marriages being held on the island, most of the island's population gathered the following morning on the pier to bid the couple farewell on their honeymoon.
Christina stood there with her husband John, both feeling pride and joy at the happy occasion. Jeannie MacKay sat on a wheelchair and waved them goodbye, with Alex moving her into a good position to wave them off.

The ferry honked its horn as was the tradition, as they set off for their honeymoon.

Malcolm and Janice, as did much of the island, wondered how the Captain and Big Duncan managed the trip across the water safely, but with their cargo safely delivered to Sconser, the Captain made a point of coming down to bid them farewell before they drove off the ferry. It really was just a ruse while big Duncan tied some cans to their rear bumper and attempted quickly to spray the words *Just Married* on the boot. Running out of time, he had to shorten the phrase, and all he could do was simply add an apostrophe at where he thought was an appropriate place.

As the couple drove down the A82, Malcolm had joked that it was Paisley they were going to, but as they drove through that area on the road to Glasgow Airport, he told his wife that their intended destination was in fact Paris.

As he reflected on the events of the last nine months, he thought that Duncan's misspelt graffiti on the car summed it up best. It was after all

Just Ma'd